TOP
OF THE
WORLD

This is a new edition of a quite extraordinary book which has now been published in twenty-two countries and has sold nearly 1,000,000 copies. It is a novel of adventure and danger and courage among a primitive people. But though it is fiction, the social, sexual and alimentary habits of its characters, the religious beliefs, medical practices and other modes and manners are sober anthropological facts.

". . . its people, strange as they are, become real. They are also likable, even lovable, with a gift for happiness and humor as well as realism. This story has a fascination of the unusual."

—*New York Herald Tribune*

"Mr. Ruesch, who is a very skillful writer, tells about the Eskimos with affection and humor and makes them seem a very sensible and attractive people, although their way of living is not for everybody, of course."

—*The New Yorker*

TOP OF THE WORLD was originally published in the United States by Harper & Row. It was the basis for the motion picture *The Savage Innocents* produced by Magic Films, starring Anthony Quinn and Yoko Tani and directed by Nicholas Ray.

TOP

OF THE

WORLD

by Hans Ruesch

ORIGINAL EDITION:
HARPER + ROW 1950

PUBLISHED BY POCKET BOOKS · NEW YORK

1951

TOP OF THE WORLD

Harper & Row edition published February, 1950

A *Pocket Book* edition
1st   printing.........March, 1951
7th   printing........August, 1968

Chapters of this book have appeared in the following magazines:
Liberty, November, 1946; *Collier's,* October, 1944, and
April, 1947; *Argosy,* November, 1946; *Saturday Evening Post,* June, 1945.

Top of the World has also been published in the following countries:
Argentina, Belgium, Denmark, England, France, Germany, Hungary,
Israel, Italy, The Netherlands, Norway, Portugal, Sweden,
Switzerland and Yugoslavia.

This *Pocket Book* edition includes every word
contained in the original, higher-priced edition. It is printed
from brand-new plates made from completely reset, clear, easy-to-read
type. *Pocket Book* editions are published by Pocket Books, a division
of Simon & Schuster, Inc., 630 Fifth Avenue, New York, N.Y. 10020.
Trademarks registered in the United States and other countries.

L

CONTENTS

CONTENTS

COLD FACTS

As each appearance of one of my Eskimo stories, in an American magazine or abroad, has entailed a deluge of letters inquiring whether the background I used had any factual base, I now wish to state beforehand that the social, sexual, and alimentary habits, the religious beliefs, the medical practices, and other modes and manners described in this book, though it sails under the flag of fiction, are sober anthropological facts, applying chiefly to the Central Eskimos. They are corroborated (with due allowances for regional and tribal variations) by men such as Fritjof Nansen, Kai Birket-Smith, Knud Rasmussen, Peter Freuchen, Franz Boas, G. de Poncins, and other recognized authorities on the Arctic and its inhabitants. I strongly recommend their reports to anyone interested in documentary evidence on the subject, which is beyond the purpose of this novel.

The Eskimos' buoyant happiness and gaiety is as undenied as it is unexplained; some choose to attribute it to their vivifying diet. The occasional clashes of Christian missionaries with the native population, as well as the assumption of modern scientists that deposits of uranium ore exist under the Arctic icecap, are not merely convenient inventions designed to heighten the drama of a story. The case of the Eskimo who ate his own frozen feet in order to survive—and succeeded—is an occurrence which found its way into the daily press.

H.R.

PART I

CHAPTER ONE

•

The Men

WHEN Ernenek raised his head from the sleeping bag his thoughts usually ran at once to the heap of fish and meat rotting into tenderness behind the seal oil lamp.

But not today.

Today, seeing Siksik bent over her husband's bearskins in a corner of the little igloo, he made a sudden resolution before lending an ear to the demands of his stomach. Since he contributed more than his share to the sustenance of the little household he was going to demand a full share in Anarvik's marital rights also, so that he no longer would have to ask permission each time he felt like laughing a little with Siksik, or when he needed new mittens sewn or his boots mended. He would at last have a wife of his own to order around—something he had never known, because he was young, and because here in the farthest North, woman was as scarce as bear was plentiful. But Ernenek knew the importance of a wife of one's own—to scrape one's skins and sew one's garments and to listen to one's jokes during the night.

Especially when the night lasts six months.

Even now he would have liked exchanging a little laughter with Siksik before leaving for the hunt. But he knew right from wrong as well as any man, and so he knew it would be most improper to avail oneself of another man's wife without first asking the husband's permission.

And Ernenek seldom did anything improper.

1

But he was tired of asking. Not that Anarvik ever refused: refusing the loan of a wife or a knife was a sign of intolerable meanness. Yet also, constantly asking favors was undignified for someone belonging to a race so proud that they call themselves simply Inuits, or Men, implying that all others aren't, by comparison, real men; even if the rest of the world has chosen to call them Eskimos—from an Algonquin word meaning Eaters-of-Raw-Meat—whether in mockery or envy has not been established.

Siksik had prepared tea on the soapstone cooking lamp. She filled a bowl and, waddling pigeon-toed owing to the boots of ringed seal that reached up to her crotch, offered Ernenek the drink with a smile. Man and woman dressed in this identical fashion. Both were stodgy and muscular and with the same joyful, broad and flat face, looking alike except for their hair, which Ernenek wore long and unruly while Siksik's rose in a neat turret-shaped coiffure on the top of her head, shining with blubber and pinned with fishbones.

"Where is Anarvik?" Ernenek inquired.

"It is not impossible that he went sealing in the Bay of the Blind Walrus. It came to pass that one sleep ago you and he guzzled a whole seal," she added with a giggle, and Ernenek responded with the easy and ever-ready laughter of his race.

The tea was warm, which was too hot for him. He couldn't drink anything warm. He blew on it, gazing at the woman over the rim of his bowl. Then he drank, ate the tea leaves and crawled out of his bag. Over his jacket suit of birdskins with the down turned inside he donned a suit of bearhide with the hair outside and tucked the trousers into his sealskin boots. Stooping under the vaulted ice wall he cut himself big chunks of rotted meat with his circular knife and crammed them into his mouth with the palm of his hand.

Crawling out of the narrow tunnel on all fours he pulled

along the leader of the dozing huskies, and the rest of the team followed, yawning and shaking the hoarfrost from their thick pelts. Soon they were yapping for food, baring their teeth (that had been flattened with stones lest they should gnaw through their traces), all bearing more likeness to wolves than dogs, with pointed snouts and glaring yellow eyes.

Ernenek iced the runners and lashed the sled. Then he harnessed the dogs, made sure they all wore the little shoes designed to protect their feet from the sharpness of the ice and the salt of the sea, retrieved the sled anchor and stepped aboard. Under the whip the dogs spread fanwise behind their leader, tearing at the traces by which each of them was individually tied to the sled and yelping after the white puffs of smoke from their muzzles.

It was warm, perhaps thirty below freezing, and Ernenek didn't have to trot after the sled for warmth, but could sit on it luxuriously enjoying the ride. The southern sky, reflecting an absent sun, was a mild blue that shaded into a tender purple in the north. Under this pallid heaven the earth appeared flat and bloodless, with neither shades nor hues, as to the eyes of dogs that make no distinction between colors.

The Glacial Ocean on which he traveled, frozen deeper than a man is tall and stingily carpeted with snow, showed clearly the tracks of Anarvik's sled. To the right were low bluffs and hills, white and dead. To the left, only the haze of spring bounded the ocean.

Ernenek never turned to glance at the solitary igloo he was leaving behind—tiny blister of ice on the roof of the world. His thoughts were racing ahead to the next island's great bay where Anarvik had gone sealing. He had even neglected to take blubber with him for fuel and light—the traveler's first rule. He was too much concerned with his question.

There were two answers to every question, and each had

3

its risks. That much Ernenek knew. If Anarvik's answer was Yes, Ernenek would lose considerable face for being granted still another favor. Anarvik was proud, a real man, and it would be quite like him to mortify Ernenek with a ready acceptance of his request. To get even with him Ernenek would then have to double his hunting efforts in order to mortify his partner in his turn with endless gifts of food.

If the answer was No, Ernenek could indeed jeer at his friend over *his* loss of face, but it would be a small consolation for having to look elsewhere for a mate, traveling uncomfortably alone, perhaps a year to the southward, where the sun and the women come from, and the land is peopled by tribes whose ways are foreign to a Polar Eskimo, and therefore distasteful to him. Any way you looked at it, life would be fraught with hazards once the question had fallen.

And yet it could be postponed no longer: for two years now Anarvik had been announcing the impending arrival of his brother Ooloolik. "He has two growing daughters and you may take your choice," Anarvik had pointed out, laughing. But the seasons had come and gone, Ernenek had waited in vain, and Anarvik had merely shrugged and said, "He may come end of next winter."

A winter more or a winter less seemed unimportant to Anarvik who had seen many. But not to Ernenek who had seen few. What if Ooloolik never came? He may have changed his mind. Or be dead. Or others may have taken his daughters.

And Ernenek was tired of waiting.

Anarvik's sled appeared as a little pin point on the great expanse and Ernenek spurred his team with whip and shout. Slowly the pin point grew to a line, then the sled became visible, then Anarvik and his dogs. The dogs were in an uproar, pulling furiously at their leashes.

Ernenek flung the sled anchor overboard, fastened the team and swaggered over the frozen sea. For all his impatience he trod the ice softly, by dint of habit, lest he frighten away the seal below. Anarvik, kneeling on a caribou skin so as not to freeze fast to the ground, had his back to him.

"A man has something to ask," Ernenek said with a scowl.

"Quiet!" said Anarvik without turning his head. "A man at work can't listen to questions. One thing at a time."

Deflated, Ernenek stopped beside him, curious to see what he was doing. Anarvik was busy with his flint knife but was ever again focusing his attention on a white shape ahead. The shape was a huge bear.

And the bear was hungry.

Months of lean hunting had whittled down the flesh accumulated during the summer season and his long winter pelt hung loosely about his fatless haunches. The Polar bear didn't hibernate. While all life migrated to the southward or holed up in igloos and lairs for rest and warmth, he alone stayed abroad all winter, hunting and fishing indefatigably for himself and his mate that dropped her young in a cave dug out in the ice crust of the sea.

A while back, on one of his inland forays, this bear had smelled out an ermine mother from her lair, torn her asunder and devoured her together with the pulsing litter in her belly. Now with whetted hunger he was observing the two men. But he was uneasy.

In this region all life was exclusively carnivorous. Bear was man's biggest prize. Man was bear's biggest prize. Here it had not yet been decided whether man or bear was the crown of creation.

"It is not impossible that someone will fell a bear," said Anarvik.

Shivering with the lust of the hunt Ernenek knelt beside him. "Let us set the dogs on him and finish quickly."

Anarvik shook his head. "He might kill many dogs, and we have none to spare. No, Ernenek. Somebody will get the bear in the usual, proven fashion."

Circling and sniffing, the bear was slowly moving closer.

With his flint knife Anarvik had carved a long splint from his whalerib bow and sharpened the ends. He coiled the splint in his hand and released it suddenly to test its resilience. Then he pulled out a chunk of blubber he had been warming within his clothes, against his stomach. He kneaded the blubber into a ball, swiftly, before it could freeze, and pressed the tightly coiled whalebone splint into it. The blubber ball hardened instantly on the ice.

He began moving forward on all fours and the bear withdrew growling, with little jumps, throwing up his shaggy hindquarters and leering over his shoulder. Anarvik stopped and called to him with motions and cooing sounds, and the bear returned tentatively, in a half-circle. Anarvik's sparse mustache quivered as he rolled the spring bait forcefully over the thin blanket of snow.

The yellow ball came to a halt a few paces from the bear. Puzzled, he approached cautiously, stretching out his nose forward and whimpering a little in uncertainty. Hunger told him to eat; another instinct, deeper and more mysterious, told him to distrust whatever came from those little beings, so frighteningly purposeful.

Anarvik waited flat and motionless, arms and legs spread out. Behind him Ernenek breathlessly watched the bear put out a long blue tongue and lick the bait, retire, lick again, and staunchly retire again. But it was impossible to resist temptation forever. Bear are only human. With a billowy movement, his snout suddenly shot forward and engulfed the bait, dropping it into the bottomless pit of his belly.

Simultaneously, Anarvik and Ernenek leaped to their

feet with cheers and laughter, for the bear was theirs.
Almost.

At the men's sudden outburst the bear backed up. Mystified, he began to circle, then sat down on his haunches
and studied them for a while. Finally, he began closing in.

The men were preparing to retreat when suddenly he
jumped up and gave a long anguished moan that ran unchecked over the great sea, silencing the dogs, then bucked
about and growled savagely.

"In his stomach the blubber has melted," cried Anarvik
triumphantly.

"And the blade has sprung open!"

All at once the bear turned on his heels and shuffled off
yammering.

Dusk was dimming already, for day was short as yet,
lighting the roof of the world for but a few hours with
each turn of the sun. Without a word Anarvik and Ernenek gripped their spears and started after their quarry,
glancing at each other and laughing, just laughing with the
glee of the hunt, everything else forgotten.

Stumbling and wailing the bear drifted coastward, as the
men moved to cut off his retreat toward the sea fields, his
element and abode. After reaching the first foothills of the
land he began to stop frequently and look over his shoulder
to see if the chase was still on, threads of spittle dangling
on his chest. His lair must be near by, but he wouldn't
lead the hunters there. Reluctantly he moved on, up the
frozen hillsides.

The soles of his feet, covered with close-set hair, enabled
him to walk securely on the ice, while the men's boots had
a poor grip on the slippery slopes. And they had to take
heed not to work themselves into a sweat, which meant
freezing to death. But the bear's course was wayward and
erratic and the men could keep up with him covering only
half as much ground.

It grew colder on the heights, fifty or sixty below, and the beloved gale blew, and Anarvik and Ernenek were happy because they hunted. Never for an instant did they worry about the forsaken provisions, and the dogs, and the woman. They were not hungry at the moment; the dogs were always hungry anyhow, whether they were fed or not; and the woman would manage somehow, as women always did. This was the Hunt—the very essence of life.

They ate nothing but the bear's droppings that were streaked with blood, and after the beast was gutted of everything but fear and pain, and hunger came knocking at the walls of their stomachs, Ernenek said:

"Somebody is hungry." These were the first words spoken since the chase had started.

Anarvik nodded his agreement.

But never for a moment did they consider turning back.

When day had once more risen tentatively, a gale pouring in from the Glacial Ocean churned up the shallow snow, turning the pallid heaven a murky gray, and for a space they lost sight of their quarry in the blinding blizzard and plunged forth in sudden alarm.

They were led back to the bear by his laments and almost crashed into him, and both men contrived to give him a good poke in the ribs with their horn-tipped spears to let him know he wasn't dreaming. A snarl of rage rose from the huge shadow fumbling upright in the snow swirl and drowned off in the wind, and from there on they stuck so close to their quarry that they could smell it—smell the bitter odor of fear emanating from its pelt.

A few times the bear wheeled about in rage and charged; they then waddled off in a hurry, whining in terror, stumbling and slipping downhill, until the bear sat down on his haunches, wagging his head; and the instant danger was past, the men laughed.

8

The second night was the worst. The blizzard thickened, forcing them to follow the bear too close at the heels for comfort, and the pangs of hunger hammered with mounting intensity, weakening their knees and increasing the danger of perspiration, while the bear, that seemed to have a hundred lives, kept trekking his furious trek up and down the forbidding slopes.

But when hunger and the raging blizzard had called on the men, their minds had cast an anchor across the ocean to the distant igloo, safe and tender and warm. The intimate amber light; the charnel heap of meat and fish rotting behind the lamp; the quiet sound of hides being scraped and of caribou sinew being needled through boots and garments. . . .

Once they came within a brief march of one of the meat caches which they kept scattered on land and sea.

"Maybe he goes off that way," Anarvik said. "Then one of us can get provisions."

They tried to drive the bear in the right direction, without success. He knew nothing about the cache.

When this hope was blighted it had been four days since they had had sleep and food, and their will had to make up for the dwindling forces of their bodies. And since the thought of giving up the hunt never for an instant entered their minds, survival became irrevocably linked with the capture of the bear, and the lust of the chase was exalted by the animal fear of doom.

They lost notion of time till the blizzard abated, revealing that a new day had risen. They were high up on the bluffs, dominating the frozen sea. In the south the sky was luminous and the silent earth seemed mellow and soft with the promise of spring.

By this time the bear was very sick. In his lumbering fashion he jogged on laboriously, dragging on the ground a head that had grown too heavy. Sometimes slipping and stumbling to their knees the men followed stonily, their laughter gone, the lines of strain marking their greased faces, their eyes red and rimmed with rime. Hunger had departed. Stomachs had gone to sleep. They did not even scoop up handfuls of snow any longer. Their mouths were set, their bellies forgotten, and in their very minds all thoughts and memories had perished. Between skin and flesh, fat had been burning away incessantly, unreplaced, their motion no longer warmed them and they shivered a little, the cold knifing noticeably down their throats with every breath.

And still, could there be anything greater than this—chasing the white bear over the top of the world?

The end came suddenly. All at once the bear gave up. As though he had decided that if he had to die he might as well die with dignity, he squatted on his hindquarters, put his forepaws in his lap, and waited. Round his neck was a pink napkin of frozen froth. He held his ears flat and his teeth bared as in a sneer. No longer did he cry. Only the white clouds of respiration came fast and raspy and his little bloodshot eyes moved helplessly.

The two men closed in slowly, Ernenek from the front and Anarvik from the side, ready to jump if he pawed. The bear grabbed Anarvik's spear and broke it like a straw the instant Ernenek speared him clean through the top of the throat, below the jaw, where the pelt was thinnest.

They barely ate after the kill, their stomachs fast asleep by now, and being too eager to show off their prize intact at home. Ernenek only sucked the blood from the wound, for strength, though it badly scalded his lips, and Anarvik sucked the brain from a little hole made in the nape of the neck. Then they separated the innards before they froze, lugged their kill down the slopes to the sea, cached it in the snow by the shore and happily trudged off.

In a straight line it took them half a turn of the sun to

regain their sleds, laughing uproariously on the way and slapping each other's big backs. If the famished dogs had not devoured one another it was only due to the bluntness of their teeth, but they had battled furiously over the skinful of fish on Anarvik's sled and some were licking the frozen gore of their wounds.

The men's appetites had been aroused by the taste of the brain and the blood, and all the way to the cached quarry and all the way back home they chewed on bits of sealskin to stay the pangs of hunger lest they should begin eating their kill.

During their absence a second igloo had mushroomed beside theirs and unknown puppies were playing before the tunnel.

Siksik emerged, followed by Anarvik's brother, Ooloolik, who had at last arrived with his wife Powtee and his two marriageable daughters, Imina and Asiak.

It was a noisy arrival, for seven is a crowd. At first they exchanged greetings with a good deal of ceremony, each trying to outgrin the other while bowing and shaking hands high above their heads; then they rubbed wrinkling noses. This done, Ooloolik's family paid unstinted compliments to the kill with such outcries as, "It is not small!"—while the hunters belittled it with all their power, to show they were capable of quite other deeds: "It is only a cub; nobody wanted to kill it but it insisted on being caught."

Then everybody crawled into Anarvik's igloo.

To the bear's spleen, hung up on a pole, a knife and a sewing needle were added as a present to the dead bear, so that his soul might tell the others of the excellent treatment it had received, making them eager to be killed in their turn.

Then the banquet began.

They ate all night, nibbling at the provisions in the larder while waiting for the bear to thaw. Anarvik skinned

11

it as soon as the pelt had softened. The pelt belonged to him, for he had sighted the bear, but as Ernenek expressed his admiration for it Anarvik humiliated him by letting him have it.

The liver belonged to Ernenek, for he had done the killing, and as soon as it had thawed he presented Anarvik with it in order to get even with him. Anarvik couldn't endure this humiliation and passed the liver on to Powtee who, dutiful wife as she was, handed it to Ooloolik. But Ooloolik gallantly offered it to Siksik, who returned it to Ernenek, who tried it on the two girls, who were too young to accept it.

Nevertheless, they managed to dispose of the liver pretty quickly once Ooloolik, his appetite suddenly getting the better of his manners, took a mighty bite out of it, and everybody plunged in almost simultaneously, with teeth and knives. Ernenek caused long, lusty yells of laughter when in his eagerness he gashed Powtee's cheek with his knife while she tore at the liver with what teeth were left in her old mouth.

In high spirits they ate their way through all the tender innards, while the tougher cuts were added to the charnel heap to rot and mellow and the tongue was hung up to dry in the smoke of the lamp.

They alternated the sweet bear meat with green, moldy marrow and rank tallow that they washed down with swills of tea, careful not to touch fish while eating meat, lest they should arouse the ire of the spirits. And the little igloo was all and more than the men had pictured during the chase: filled to the roof with feasting people while dogs and puppies crawled between their legs; the circular, blood-stained ice wall mirroring the salmon-colored flame of the wick that floated in the melting blubber; the rich odor of fresh bear meat, heavy and sweet, mingling with the subtle fragrance of decay; the ice resonant with the sound of gnawing and gulping and the cracking of bones, of jest and fat laughter.

The more Anarvik and Ernenek ate, the hungrier they became. Stripped to the waist and radiant with happiness and warmth they kept glutting themselves, spreading round the belt, their faces dripping with blood. When they felt too heavy to lift a hand they lay down on their backs and allowed the women to drop choice morsels into their mouths and pour tea down their throats between one belch and the next.

This was the life!

With eyes afloat in laughter Ernenek looked from one of Ooloolik's daughters to the other as they hovered over him with tidbits and smiles. These were women who knew how a man should be treated, and they certainly knew also how to scrape hides and sew boots and do other little things for him. But which one to choose he couldn't decide. Imina was prettier, but Asiak's laughter was warmer.

Ernenek felt completely contented, and at peace with the world. When he was unable to swallow, he closed eyes and mouth and the hubbub around him washed away. He would give the food time to settle and then be ready for more. He stretched out his hand to make sure that Anarvik was at his side.

There he was, already snoring like a litter of walruses.

It dimly occurred to Ernenek there was something he wanted to ask him. That's what he had set out for, a few turns of the sun ago. But in vain did he strain his memory.

The thought was dead, and buried, and forgotten.

CHAPTER TWO

Woman Hunt

AFTER growing periods of daylight the sun once more circled the sky during all of the twenty-four hours, and although it never rose very high and all the shadows were long, owing to the slanting rays, yet the brilliance of the ice accounted for a glaring light, while the length of the day made for weather that was unbearably hot for the Polar Eskimos even if it never succeeded in thawing the sea.

Any man would have realized that the mere arrival of Kidok, a tall, gay, swaggering trader, who without delay began humming around Ooloolik's daughters, meant high time for a quick decision.

Any man but Ernenek.

He was a stiff hunter but a poor lover. He knew how to slay the big bear and to spear the great seal, but woman was too heavy a game for him. He only reflected sadly that such was life: sometimes for years nobody drops in; then altogether, within the same season, two or even three parties may arrive—and a man has a dilemma big as a whale.

All summer Ernenek gallivanted indiscriminately with both Imina and Asiak, who warded him off jestingly but valiantly; until, returning from a solitary hunting trip when already the sun was on the wane, he saw a small dash on the white horizon, meaning a team and sled, someone coming or someone going, a great event whichever way you looked at it.

He lugged the blood-dripping kill from his sled and crawled into the igloo. Anarvik and Ooloolik were drinking tea with their wives and Asiak. But Imina was missing.

"It came to pass that Kidok left," Ooloolik announced, "taking along somebody's worthless daughter for his wife. You couldn't make up your mind, so he did."

Everyone laughed except Ernenek, who stood quite still, his jaw dropping, bafflement in his dark almond eyes. At length he blurted out:

"But it happens that somebody wanted Imina, and is going to get her back and kill the thief!"

"He gave us a new saw," said Anarvik, hinting that the marriage was legal, and Powtee added:

"Why don't you take our little Asiak? She is just as worthless, of course, but there is nothing Imina can do for you that Asiak can't."

Asiak blushed and snickered and hid her face behind her fist, but Ernenek stamped his foot.

"Somebody wants Imina and not Asiak!"

Siksik shrugged. "She was yours for the asking."

Ernenek spat angrily and plunged into the tunnel, and the whole group crawled out after him, infected by his excitement, but laughing.

"Somebody's team is tired, but still much faster than Kidok's. It will be easy to catch him."

But he didn't start without considerable delay. He reharnessed the team and inspected their shoes, shouting orders and pleas to haul more provisions onto his sled, and there was vast excitement in the camp, everybody waddling about pigeon-toed, shouting and laughing.

When sled and dogs were ready Ernenek decided he was thirsty and crawled back in for a bowl of tea. Regardless of his haste the brew stayed long hot, and testing it with his fingers he scalded himself and hopped up and down, cursing. While waiting for the tea to cool he stuffed his face with frozen fish, talking between mouthfuls—mainly to himself, as was his wont.

"Somebody will stick an ice knife in Kidok's stomach and pull out his liver, cut his ears off and stuff them down his throat. Then cut his head off and put it on top of his body, cut his eyes out and put them on top of his head. That will teach him to steal!"

Anarvik lifted a warning finger. "If you kill him, nobody will ever admit you into his igloo again."

"Not even you?"

"Not even I."

This set Ernenek reflecting, which was not becoming to him: it put a heavy scowl on his otherwise unruffled face. Expulsion from the community was the only penalty in a land where there existed neither laws nor judges nor chiefs; and although human company was prized as highly as life itself, Ernenek was surprised that simple murder should entail so stiff a retribution, for he saw nothing wrong in it. It was what any young seal would do, attacking one of the aging bulls for the possession of the female.

And what was good enough for the seal was good enough for Ernenek.

"If that's the way you feel about it," he finally said, sulkily, "somebody will just take Imina back and give Kidok a clubbing to remember. But if he puts up resistance, he shall be killed like a seal!"

"If you can't help killing him, don't neglect to eat a little piece of his liver to conciliate his ghost and make it harmless," said Anarvik, a man of vast experience. "An angry ghost is very dangerous."

By now the tea was cool. Ernenek guzzled it noisily, along with a few slices of frozen fish, smacked his lips, and crawled out. Although his huskies uproariously proclaimed their hunger he forbore feeding them, for starved dogs are fast dogs. The team howled and yapped angrily as he climbed onto the biggest bundle.

"Take Asiak along," Ooloolik said, pushing forward his giggling daughter. "It will make your bargain with Kidok easier. He paid for one of our worthless daughters, and he shall have one."

Ernenek hesitated for a moment before waving her aboard. She had barely seated herself when he whipped the dogs and they fanned out, yawling and yelping.

Kidok's sled had shrunk to a pin point on the white expanse of snow blanketing thinly the Glacial Ocean. This region was too cold for much precipitation, even in summertime. Here and there in the midst of the flat sea some submarine storm or strong set of currents had lifted the petrified waters in clusters of weird forms and shapes like some legendary ghost city of wrecked skyscrapers. In the distance was land, capped with snow, cut by ridges of naked rock that stood out dead and dark against a pale-green heaven. It was hot, only some ten or fifteen below, and Ernenek had stripped to the waist, baring his powerful chest to the wind. He had left behind his outer suit of bearhide and wore only his inner garment of birdskins.

"In a little while somebody will have caught up with Kidok," Ernenek boasted, after the team's initial excitement had abated and he could hear himself talk.

"It is possible," said Asiak, sitting placidly behind him with her arms crossed on her chest, "that by then Kidok will have covered just as much ground."

Time was measured by the progress of the sun that floated pallidly over the edge of the horizon, rising a little higher at noon, sinking a little lower at midnight. Yet at all hours the watery sunlight reflected by the ice was dazzling and the travelers wore goggles made of a strap of wood with a slit for each eye and had blackened their eyelids and nostrils with soot to break the glare.

But the sun was sagging a little more at each turn, soon it would disappear, and over the top of the world night would come, and stay.

"Why do you want to catch up with Kidok?" Asiak asked blandly after a little while.

"To get Imina. Don't you know that?"

"Somebody knows only that you will be everybody's laughing stock for years and years to come. Who has ever heard of a man running after a woman! And as you know, the seal like to be caught only by men who are successful with women, and you will see that as soon as word of this chase spreads around among them they will despise and avoid you."

"Just a superstitious woman making a lot of wind!" Erneñek said angrily, whipping his huskies one by one. "I know full well what to do so the seal might never hear of it."

After the sun had made half a turn around them the team showed signs of fatigue, panting more and pulling less and stumbling frequently, but the pin point they pursued was rapidly growing.

"He must have stopped to rest his team," Ernenek said, squinting.

"And our team is also getting tired."

But Ernenek substituted the whip for food and rest, till the huskies swayed and floundered, stepping over one another to escape the lash and entangling their traces, and he had to halt and unravel them. They growled and snatched for his mitts and he put them in their places with kicks and slaps. When he fed them scanty chunks of frozen fish they gulped them whole, with bones and all, battling savagely and entangling their traces anew, and he had to straighten them out again. Then he gnawed from the same fish and tossed some to Asiak.

By now the huskies had dropped on their bellies, hiding their noses in their forepaws and refusing to budge, and Ernenek grew weary trying to work reason into them with a club.

"We may have to let them rest," Asiak ventured.

Ernenek bounced up and down on his feet with impatience, and so that the stop might not be wasted he decided to re-ice the runners. He unloaded the sled and turned it over, always muttering to himself. He stopped only to melt snow in his mouth and squirt it on a foxtail that he ran over the runners, rapidly following up with his mitten to make the coating of ice even. After reloading the sled he abruptly decided he was tired.

He went down for a nap and asked to be wakened sometime soon.

When he woke it was of his own accord. The dogs were bristling heaps of hoarfrost in the snow, Asiak was slumbering placidly, the sun had rolled to the opposite side of the horizon, and Kidok's sled had treacherously slipped out of the picture.

Ernenek cursed and spat and jumped about frantically, booted his team into sudden activity, and before Asiak could rub the dreams from her eyes the chase was on again.

They rode on over the ocean in the tracks of Kidok's runners, eating on the sled, and scooping up snow on the run for drink, as the huskies did. When at length Kidok's sled came into sight again Ernenek gave out a roar of joy.

"Why are you chasing him?" Asiak asked languidly.

"You must be stupid or deaf, woman," Ernenek said irritably. "Somebody has told you before: to get Imina!"

The situation didn't change except for the larder getting low. The heat wave passed, the air became breathable again, some thirty or forty below, and sometimes there was a gust of frosty wind, reminding Ernenek of his beloved winter gale, and he muttered volubly to himself as whenever he was in good humor.

Or in bad humor, for that matter.

He grew excited discovering that Kidok had halted. Coming closer he saw the reason for the halt: Kidok was fishing. He had cut a hole in the ocean and now, bent over the hole, his fish spear strike-ready, was peering into the depths, his behind in the air and his nose almost touching the surface of the sea which had filled the hole after the ice had been extracted. He turned his head quickly when his team sounded the alarm, but reverted to his occupation till the last moment, when Ernenek's sled raced in on him. Then he jumped up, rushed to the sled that Imina was holding ready, and off they went like flakes in a blizzard.

Ernenek swept past the fish hole with shouts of encouragement and cracking whip. But all at once he stopped his team. There was the head of a huge trout by the hole, the flesh showing blood red, and smaller heads and bones scattered about.

"What is the matter now?" Asiak asked.

Ernenek alighted and stamped from one foot to the other in indecision. "These waters contain fish that are not small."

"Kidok is no small fisherman."

"If Kidok speared one like this, somebody can spear a bigger one."

"Can you?" Asiak asked doubtfully.

"You will get proof in no time at all," Ernenek said angrily. "Kidok won't get far. But don't walk on the ice, and keep the dogs still, too, otherwise the fish will go elsewhere."

He spread a caribou skin by the hole, knelt on it, and brought his nose to the water while his back pointed skyward. In his right hand his fish spear lay poised to strike while with his left he worked the decoy that hung on a line of sinew—a small fish carved of bone that flapped its fins when he jerked the line.

Ernenek was too engrossed to notice how much time passed. Big lucent fish were moving leisurely in the pure gloom of the ocean.

At length one was baited to the surface. Ernenek lowered his spear gently, then struck, and drew it back vibrating with the twists of a black salmon that he flung on the ice. The salmon gasped, flapped itself over and froze into stillness. Laughing, Ernenek weighed it in his hand and tossed it to Asiak.

But Asiak shrugged. "It is not big. You will never get one like Kidok, so don't waste any more time if you want to catch him."

Ernenek glanced over the ocean. "He hasn't gone far and it will be easier to catch up with him when the dogs are rested." And he lowered his nose to the water again.

Seated on the sled, feet dangling, Asiak smiled with her round, pleasant cheeks bursting with fat. With the point of her snow knife she boned the salmon and munched it slowly, smiling dreamily to herself.

Time went by and also fish went by but Ernenek failed to catch them. He could see them floating or squirming in the dark depths, alone or in pairs or in shoals, but none came quite within striking distance; and once a whole shoal did, he gave a wild thrust, trying to spear several at once, and they scattered, unharmed.

"You made a hole in the water," Asiak said. "Somebody heard the fish laugh."

This made Ernenek angry and he decided to leave.

The temperature dropped further. The huskies trotted nose down, following the scent, and Ernenek and Asiak could take catnaps on the sled. They needed little sleep in summer, saving it up for the long winter night. But sometimes they had to rest the team. Then Ernenek would cut a hole in the ocean with his ice chisel or his saw and spear some fish, and once, when they were not far from the shore, he slew a fox with an arrow. Asiak prepared it, serving the tender innards as soon as they had cooled, putting the harder flesh aside to season and keeping the hide as a mop.

It was the fox, with the first white hair in its coat, that heralded the approaching winter more than the darkening world to which their eyes gradually grew adjusted, and the first glacial breeze brought shivers of delight to Ernenek's exposed body. His good humor was back and there was a lot of jesting. Asiak teased him about his team that never in a hundred summers would reach the other sled, and about his catch that never could compare with Kidok's fish, the heads and bones of which were scattered alongside the tracks. He repaid her, saying she didn't know how to lash a sled, for the traces she had fitted while he was busy spearing their luncheon frequently broke and, as a rule, just when Kidok's sled had grown big and approachable.

One of the bitches whelped on the trail. She had been tied with the shortest trace so that her teammates might not swallow up the litter, and Asiak bent down in full run and one by one picked up the fuming bundles. With her teeth she tore apart the first five wrappings, which were cool where they had lain in the snow and scalding hot above, and spilled the jelly and the sticky, sweet-tasting skin over the edge of the sled, and slipped the damp pups into her inner jacket. A bitch on the trail could raise no more, and Asiak didn't open the next four that were dropped but kept them on the sled for use as dog feed. They hardened quickly in the wind of the ride.

The sun had made several turns, perhaps seven or eight —it did not matter exactly how many where time was long —when a blizzard broke and Ernenek began talking to himself in great excitement.

Darkness narrowed the horizon. A gale descending from the distant heights swept the Glacial Ocean, raising murky clouds of snowdust from the ground and driving them horizontally over the great expanse, and Ernenek and Asiak added blubber to their faces and squinted and bent against the weather. Kidok's sled dropped out of sight once more, the huskies were not agreed on the scent, and Ernenek had to halt and dismount several times till he had uncovered with his heel the tracks that had vanished under the drifting snow.

Sled and team swayed under the pressure of the wind and Ernenek began to miss his outer coat with the big hood that left only the eyes exposed. Ice clung to his brow and filled his ears.

Yet he would never have halted unless there were an accident.

In order to tame the wind and punish it for its insolence Ernenek began to beat it with his whip and stick it with his knife. The wind, however, not only refused to be intimidated, but with a hurricane gust it upset the sled and swept it for hundreds of feet, scattering bundles and riders and team over the sea in a furious jumble and piling them up against an ice ridge. The huskies howled. Ernenek cursed. Asiak laughed. In vain did they try to unscramble the dogs and replace the sled on its tracks; the wind upset it again before they could load it.

"Excuse a woman for talking, but the sled might break and then you will never catch Kidok," Asiak shouted into Ernenek's snow-filled ear. "We should call a halt. If we can't travel, he can't travel either."

They pushed the sled against the ridge and cut the hopelessly entangled dog traces with their knives, and while the freed huskies huddled together, whimpering and burrowing frenziedly, Ernenek began erecting a shelter.

On a patch of packed drift snow he drew with his spear a circle barely wider than he was tall. Staying inside the circle he cut large cubes of snow from underfoot, placing them round himself on the drawn line. He cut out the cubes for the higher rows from beneath his feet, thus digging and building simultaneously. He trimmed the last cube of each row with his snow knife till it fitted snugly in the gap, making each row narrower than the one below, until a single block sufficed to seal the vault.

Outside, meanwhile, with a shovel of frozen sealskin, Asiak was stamping the harsh drift snow into a fine powder, tossing it against the igloo's growing wall and plugging with it the chinks between the cubes. The completed shelter protruded only some three or four feet from the ocean surface, spheric and compact, affording no grip to the weather; the rest was below.

Above his head Ernenek made a small hole for the smoke to escape. Then he built the snow couch and the winding tunnel, designed to admit air but no wind and capable of sheltering the team, and while Asiak hauled in provisions and household necessities and covered the couch with skins, he went outside to bury the sled. Then he crawled back into the igloo, carefully beating the ice dust from his clothes before squatting on the couch.

In the dark he heard Asiak prepare the lamp, strike a spark into the tinder of dried fungi and light the wick of moss, and as the blubber began to melt in the shallow vessel the little flame grew, making the circular wall glitter and spreading warmth. But as wind and fine snow powder kept drifting in spots through the coarse-grained wall Ernenek thawed the surface with the lamp, and as soon as he removed the flame the thaw froze, making the wall airtight.

Asiak, meanwhile, had made a drying rack above the lamp with two spears stuck into the wall and flung her wet outer suit onto it. Tugging with hands and teeth she pulled off Ernenek's soaked boots and inspected them. They had burst in two places and she dried them with snow and repaired them with the whalebone needle she carried in her hair and with caribou sinew. Then she added them to the garments on the rack.

The rack, the lamp, the larder, the block of drinking snow, the sparking flints and touchwood, and all other household implements were disposed after a pattern older than history—each item within arm's reach, to be found easily in the dark and so that any chore might be accomplished without leaving the couch. This igloo was identical with the igloo they had left and with their next igloo, and their utensils were built to fit it. Because there was not enough elbowroom, the flint ax was short and the house knife of caribou bone was circular, requiring only a movement of the wrist.

Asiak had a hundred things to do, as women have around the house. There was always some sewing to be done. The wick had to be trimmed constantly lest it go out. The garments on the rack had to be shifted. Snow for tea had to be melted. But her real work was ahead—when the dried skins would have to be scraped and chewed back into softness.

The soothing sound of stitching, the lamp's sunset-colored glow on the ice wall, and the familiar odor of the wick floating in the melting blubber made Ernenek wish to sleep. But all at once he felt uncomfortably chilly. He had wasted energy and fed insufficiently, as men will when they woo, and of course he wouldn't have been Ernenek if he hadn't forgotten something of vital importance, like proper garments. His suit was drying on the rack and he crept into his big deerskin bag, holding his feet a little higher than the rest of him so that the warm air might rise to his toes, but even this proven device did not warm him, and sleep eluded him. Usually he drew pleasure from falling asleep half frozen. But not now.

Through his eyelashes he observed Asiak. After a while she stopped sewing. She sucked at some frozen fish. She stopped the hole in the roof with a ptarmigan skin. She gave a little yawn. Then, without asking permission, she joined him in his sleeping bag.

He pretended to be slumbering soundly and ignored her intrusion. After a while the unattended wick smoked, spluttered, went out. The fury of the blizzard came muffled through the thick wall. With Asiak in the bag, warmth came, and before he knew it Ernenek was fast asleep.

He woke to the scraping of skins. The storm had eased a little. Asiak smiled, seeing him creep out of the bag. She was softening his boots with scrapers of bone, using her teeth on the hardest spots. His suit was dry.

He was famished. Cool tea was waiting for him. He washed it down along with chunks of fish and blubber. By the time he grew tired of taking food, little was left.

"Somebody will look for Kidok before he can leave again," Ernenek said, picking his teeth and licking his fingers.

"It is possible that a woman will come along. He can't be far."

A few dogs howled when stepped upon in the tunnel but most of them were too tired to take notice. The gale still was strong, the sky sullen, the temperature stiff.

Uncovering Kidok's sled tracks with their heels, squinting through the ice dust and bowing to the wind, they at last discovered a little igloo crouching under the weather and almost erased by snow drifts.

They were greeted by the growling of dogs in the tunnel. Within, Kidok's igloo was exactly like Ernenek's, with the same implements identically disposed. Kidok grinned at the visitors from out of his bag and the two sisters tittered and snuffed at each other.

"Somebody has come to take Imina back," Ernenek announced without ceremony.

"We saw you following us, but thought you wanted to play games," Kidok grinned. "You always challenged my team."

"No, it wasn't to play games, but to catch up with Imina."

"Why don't you take Asiak? Can't she scrape hides and

sew boots and do all the other little things that women do?"

"Yes, she scrapes and sews," Ernenek allowed. "But somebody wants Imina because . . ." And here he reached the limit of his wits.

It didn't occur to him that perhaps he wanted Imina merely because Kidok had taken her. Red-faced and embarrassed he reached for a piece of meat lying on the floor and cut himself a lump. The other three laughed and Ernenek grew redder and redder. As Asiak had said, it was very bad form to profess any particular interest in any particular woman.

"Nobody can force a woman," said Kidok at last, proving himself a man of greater wisdom. "Imina can go with you, if she wishes. But in that case Asiak will maybe join a worthless hunter who doesn't want to travel alone?" He glanced at Asiak and so did Ernenek.

"Certainly," said Asiak, tittering.

Ernenek frowned. He became so miserable that he had to stoop repeatedly to the larder for consolation, and the only sound from him was when he spat out the bones or sucked his fingers between helpings, while the others chatted and jested till the storm was done.

When Kidok's sled was loaded and lashed they decided to return to the igloo for a last bowl of tea and another chat and another batch of jokes, which meant about another week.

There never were farewells; only arrivals were cause for celebrations. Separations are sad where companionship is rare, and departures pass unnoticed and ignored. At the most they sometimes said "Aporniakinatit" when someone left an igloo—"Now, friend, careful not to knock your head against the roof of the tunnel."

So it would have been proper for Ernenek to ignore Kidok's and Asiak's departure entirely and remain in the igloo. Instead, he followed them outside and stood by the sled with tight jaws and tragic eyes, and as the dogs tore off and the straps strained and creaked, he suddenly flung himself at the team leader, stopping the sled with such abruptness that load and passengers tumbled down pell-mell in a turmoil of yelps and curses and laughter.

Kidok picked himself up, beating his clothes, and waddled wonderingly toward Ernenek.

"Somebody would rather have Asiak after all," Ernenek blurted out miserably. "Take back Imina!"

Kidok laughed. Ernenek must have lost his wits. As if one woman wasn't as good as the next! It was all the same to Kidok, so long as Ernenek made up his mind.

He had.

For punishment he had to reload the sled, which he did with alacrity, humming gaily to himself the while, and for once he was glad to see a sled depart.

He took Asiak back to their igloo and began to sniff and paw her without wasting time. But she smacked him resonantly over the ears with a frozen salmon.

"You have chased Imina for many turns of the sun before making up your mind, and you will have to chase another worthless woman at least twice as long before she makes up hers," she said, half angry, half amused. "It is possible that a silly woman is not so easy to fell as a bear."

Ernenek was crestfallen at the unexpected turn of events, and greatly alarmed at the thought of how the seal would take this new discomfiture of his. Then Asiak dropped a startling question.

"Why did you chase Kidok?" And since Ernenek didn't answer, she added with a little laugh, "You must be stupid, man!"

Punctured and deflated, Ernenek flopped onto the couch and reached for a fish head, mumbling to himself, wondering and marveling.

CHAPTER THREE

The Facts of Life

W HEN in the gloom of fall they rejoined camp Ernenek let Asiak's parents have a lamp and they let him have Asiak.

He was proud that as a married man he now was in a position to repay other husbands for what little favors he had received from them. When he discreetly left the igloo, hinting that Anarvik might welcome a little laugh with Asiak, there was a new tilt to his head and a new square-ness to his shoulders. At last, Ernenek was a full-fledged Man. He did not allow Siksik to be a spoilsport, ignoring her insinuations that for many seasons now Anarvik had been unable to laugh or even just titter with a woman.

Old Ooloolik died the following winter for no particular reason at all. He went to sleep and forgot to wake up. This was unfortunate. If his relatives had had an inkling of his impending death they could have dressed him in his burial clothes and moved him into a makeshift shelter, as the shade of the deceased contaminates an igloo and it has to be abandoned. So in the dead of the night they decamped, erasing their tracks as they went, and built fresh igloos far enough to be safe from the dead man's vengeance; even Ernenek, who was afraid of no man living.

For a dead Eskimo is a bad Eskimo. He is enraged that he is dead while his dear ones are alive and he will hurt them with all his power. And as the dread of Ooloolik's ghost was great, the wails of mourning were loud and plentiful in an effort to conciliate it. For further precau-tion everybody built sham snares and traps about their new dwellings in order to frighten away the ghost should it want to come back.

The dead made things hard for the living. But so did the living for the dead.

Anarvik and Siksik migrated to the southward at the break of day, but Asiak's mother, Powtee, felt too old to travel, and Ernenek and Asiak stayed on with her.

They were good to the old woman who had no one left after Ooloolik had died and Imina had gone to Kidok's tribe. For a whole year they tended her with care and affection, providing her with foods and garments although her stiff fingers were unable to sew or scrape, and her teeth, used down to the gums, were incapable of softening hides any longer. They gave her choice and tender morsels, and Asiak fed her mouth to mouth, thus paying her back what she had received from her in childhood—a fair exchange. But an end would have to be set to all this, sure as winter.

And it was.

The old woman knew what it meant when she was packed on the sled and driven out over the wind-harassed ocean, luminous with stars. Nobody talked on the ride, nor when a halt was called and Ernenek made the old woman sit on a dogskin he had spread in the midst of the sea field for her, so that she might die in comfort. Embarrassed, he had then waddled back to the sled, muttering to himself and feigning to be busy with the lashings.

Asiak, to conceal her own distress, was berating the huskies more than she was wont and kicking with great accuracy at their pointed snouts when they tore at one another's pelts.

Meantime, seated composedly on the dogskin, Powtee was watching her daughter with a worried eye.

Asiak was pregnant and probably had no inkling of how close to delivery she already was. She had never witnessed human birth, nor would there be anyone with her now who had, and Powtee wondered whether her daughter had learned enough about the facts of life from the husky bitches.

"Step close, little one. A useless old woman has something to tell you."

Asiak complied and respectfully listened to her mother's words.

"It is possible that you will soon bear a child. Now you must know the child is impatient to see the world—that's why you feel it toss in your belly—and you must do everything in your power to help it on its way. If you happen to be in the igloo when the moment comes, remove the hides from the ground so as not to soil them, then stand on your knees, which is the best position for childbearing, and dig a hole under you to make room for the child. But it happens that at the last moment the child gets afraid to come out and after it has already stepped into the world it still clings to you—unlike the dogs you have seen, that are born free. So you must cut it from you, and do it immediately, otherwise it will die, and you with it. Did you understand what somebody said?"

"Almost everything. How wise you are!"

"Now listen carefully: as soon as the child is born, look if it is a boy or girl. If it is a boy, everything is all right. Lick it clean with your tongue, then rub it with blubber. Don't be afraid to rub hard: it won't break. Only after a sleep or two may you start washing it in urine. But if it is a girl you must strangle her at once, before you get fond of her, or set her out on the ice, filling her mouth with snow so that she'll die quickly."

"Why must somebody do that?"

"Because during the time you give suck to a child you will be barren, which means that in order to raise a girl you will delay the arrival of a boy, and it is indispensable that you raise a male quickly in your family: it is he that will bring in the food when you and your husband grow old, which happens very, but very quickly. Once you have a boy you may raise a girl too, if you care. But you should know that many wise parents let their daughters live only if somebody has promised already before their birth to marry them, and provide for them while they grow. Is all that clear to you, little one?"

"Yes, little one."

"Somebody is glad it is." And so as to give her daughter a chance to depart she tore her gaze away from her and stared out across the lonely white reaches and toward the distant shadows, denoting land, blurry in the gloom of the Arctic night. She was a stickler for such old rules of savoir-vivre as demanded that departures should be ignored. So it would have been as impolite for Asiak and Ernenek to take leave as for her to take notice.

But as the young couple slipped out of her life's scene, it was only in sound. In sight they stayed with her, so familiar was she with the pattern of life which was unchanged since her childhood days, and unchangeable. And she was ashamed that at the end of a full life she should not yet be satisfied with her lot, but nurture one more desire—to see and hear and hold once more in her gnarled old hands a new-born babe. And as she sat waiting for death her thoughts went to the small igloo where even now the miracle of birth was taking place. She could picture accurately everything that was happening there in her absence.

Almost everything.

Even while Powtee was waiting for death on the dogskin the child was coming to Asiak, as if speeded on its way by her great sorrow. Already during the homebound ride was she assailed by the grip of labor, though not a sound came from her lips.

Sleepy-eyed puppies emerged yapping and stumbling from the tunnel, shaking the snow from their woolly hides. While Ernenek unharnessed the team Asiak did not tarry to unload the sled, but dropped prone in the snow and with some difficulty squeezed herself through the narrow tunnel. She discarded her outer suit, lit the lamp and stretched herself out on the snow couch.

Ernenek soon followed.

His presence disturbed her. She wished to be alone in what was about to happen. "Remember," she said, keeping her eyes closed, "the musk-ox flank we cached in the great gulf last spring?"

Ernenek exulted at the memory. "It was not a small musk ox!"

"Yes, you always have the biggest everything. It must be nice and mellow now. Maybe we could eat a piece of it."

Ernenek's big face grew serious. "It is a long trip and somebody is sleepy."

"A foolish woman wants some of that meat."

Ernenek shifted his squat, powerful frame, his head slightly bent under the ice vault. "There is fat, frozen seal in the larder," he said enticingly, "and liver that is rotting since summer."

"Somebody doesn't want fat, frozen seal," Asiak said, unimpressed, "nor liver, no matter how rotted it is, but musk-ox flank."

She had had many such sudden whims lately, and it would have been easy for Ernenek to silence her with a single slap—any time he was in good shape. He often wondered why he never did it, but found no answer. There were more things Ernenek couldn't answer than one could ask. He stamped and spat and snorted and cursed. Then he added grease to his face, reharnessed the team, and off he set for a musk-ox flank.

With her foot Asiak pushed into place the snowclod that sealed the entrance, for she had chills, though up to now her pregnancy had kept her warmer than a double bear-skin; then she broke a piece of drinking snow from the block, melted it over the lamp in a vessel of hollowed soapstone and drank avidly, without ever leaving the couch. The impatient child drove daggers through her body, causing her to set her teeth while in her boots her toes curled in. The throes made her sick at her stomach and her damp hair clung to her brow. She bit her lips till they burst.

The wick of moss floating in the melting blubber of the lamp began to splutter, sending black coils of smoke toward the opening in the ceiling and calling her attention to the trimming, but she ignored it. She got up, removed the hides from the floor, and with a garment scraper gouged out a hole in the snow. She knelt over it, let her pants down to her knees and waited, resting one elbow on the couch and the other on the snow block. The apricot light mellowed, turning brown, purple, blue, gray, black.

And in the dark, Asiak's first-born dropped headlong into the snowhole.

Where there was something tugging at her she bent forward and chewed through it, and as soon as her child was free, a mighty squalling filled the igloo and she hurriedly lit the lamp to see what she had brought forth.

It was a male and the power of his voice made her guffaw a little, for it reminded her of Ernenek. She licked the soft heap of pale-brown flesh till it gleamed immaculate except for the blue Mongolic spot at the base of the spine, then dried it with a foxskin mop, smeared it with blubber, and quickly tucked it away into her deerskin bag because the pangs of the afterbirth were assailing her.

This over, she felt a reckless craving for food and wolfed a huge piece of frozen seal. After that a great quiet and contentment pervaded her. She undressed and crept into her bag.

The little hunter was squalling frantically. She stopped his mouth with her breast and he began to suck with all his might, hurting her a little but also giving her a sensation that vaguely resembled sexual pleasure.

And this also marked the reawakening of her sexual desires which, like in the animals of the wild, had gone to sleep the day of conception, causing her entire being to strive inward and to be on the defensive against the outer world.

And the long period of confinement had puzzled Ernenek who knew of the primal powers in Asiak's blood that commanded her as little as she did.

When Ernenek returned with the groceries he stayed rooted on all fours in the passageway, his big jowl unhinged, stilled in great wonder. A little crest of jet-black hair emerged from the sleeping bag beside Asiak's cheek.

"It came to pass that a woman has brought forth a child," she said shamefacedly. "But isn't he beautiful?" she added, holding it up triumphantly.

Ernenek wagged his head in doubt. "Somebody has seen bear cubs that were better looking." And he got to his feet, forgetting to beat the ice dust from his clothes.

"He will improve as he grows," Asiak said firmly. "But he has everything he needs. Even a name. His name is Papik."

"How do you know his name is Papik?" Ernenek asked, astounded.

"Because somebody happens to like that name."

So Ernenek sprawled Papik on the snow and watched him, wide-eyed, from the couch, not yet conditioned to fatherhood.

"He might not feel warm, all naked in the snow," Asiak suggested, and Ernenek lifted him up on his knees and began to inspect him from toe to top, shaking with laughter at the wee size of his parts, and Asiak felt slighted and a little angry. For, actually, the little hunter was powerfully built, with square shoulders, a big chest, short but strong arms and broad cheekbones, and his slightly slanting eyes shone black and lively in his greased face.

Ernenek made sure that every little thing was there. The tender, minute nails on the blunt-fingered hands. The short nose, almost disappearing between the bursting cheeks. The rich, round mouth and tiny tongue. . . .

"Asiak!" Ernenek rose bolt upright, hitting the ceiling and dangling his son by one foot, and the little one burst into a squall while his face grew crimson.

Asiak's eyes widened. "What is the matter?"

"It has no teeth!"

Consternation followed. Asiak probed her son's gums, unheedful of his squalls. Ernenek was right: no trace of teeth. And for the first time he saw tears on her that were not caused by laughter.

"You must have broken some taboo," he told her sternly.

"Not to my knowledge."

"Did you eat sea animals together with land animals? Or put the products of the sea and products of the land into one and the same pot?"

"Of course not."

"Then you must have tried to spear a seal, or killed a white caribou, or sewn out of season. Why don't you confess?"

"Because I didn't do it! How about your breaking some taboo? Think. Think hard!"

"A stupid woman talking thus to her husband! What is the world coming to?"

"The important thing is: what can be done about it?" She bit her finger sharply while fighting rivers; for of course she knew what had to be done.

And so did Ernenek. He shifted and coughed and cursed and muttered to himself. Then he laughed coarsely, feigning indifference.

Asiak anticipated him. "We'll set him out on the ice. The sooner the better."

Ernenek went to stroke her hair and snuff at her. "We'll have other children, and maybe they will have teeth in them."

Although a little numb from childbed, Asiak wanted to go along for the ride, and they traveled the same route they had come about one turn of the moon earlier. Powtee might still be alive, if a bear had not come to fetch her, and to Asiak the thought that little Papik would not step alone into eternity but in his grandmother's arms was somewhat of a comfort.

No bear had come to fetch the old woman and she was where they had left her, seated composedly in the midst of the white expanse like the Queen of the Sea. She was a little benumbed from such a lot of fresh air, but when finally she was able to unlock her leathery jaw it was to make a startling announcement:

"A useless old woman may know how to make his teeth grow."

It might take till summer, she explained, before the Powers of the Winds and Snows with which she, as an old woman, was on personal and excellent terms, would bow to her request; but in the end Papik would get his teeth. And although Asiak and Ernenek were not sure she knew what she was saying, for old women gibbered all sorts of things as remote from reality as the ice from the moon, they grabbed at the chance.

They drove back with her and the child, and Ernenek had to build another igloo of warm new snow leaning on and connected with their own, into which Powtee might retire with her grandchild, for she wished to be undisturbed in her conversations with the Powers of the Winds and Snows. And Asiak fretted behind the blocked entrance, waiting to be called in for the feeding.

Besides mother milk Papik got blubber to suck from Powtee's finger, and liver juice was squeezed into his mouth. The old woman barely took any nourishment herself. She became skinnier and her nose stood out more and more between the sunken and deeply furrowed cheeks. But her eyes showed more life than a brace of seal in the water.

The boy grew markedly, but as Asiak kept exploring his gums in vain, she became sullen and taciturn, and many a time Ernenek, waking to her quiet sobbing, would put out his small, rough hand from his sleeping bag and touch her wet face in the dark.

Listlessly she sewed with her triangular needle and caribou sinew the trundle hood in which to carry her son, his garments of young hide and the white boots of baby seal; listlessly she tanned the skins with human water and scraped them into softness. Whenever the north wind allowed, she stepped out into the starry night and waddled about pigeon-toed, and at times she caught herself talking aloud, like Ernenek.

Her squat but well-shaped body, grown hefty in the outdoor life of summer, fined down. This was normal in winter. But she should have got more sleep, as Ernenek and everyone else she knew did in this season. Instead, she dozed fitfully or not at all.

The little ice blister might have been a happy homestead. The igloo was small, for reasons of warmth, but it had every imaginable comfort: the larder contained plenty of blubber for fuel and light, and food enough to last all winter; and when through the thick ice wall one heard the gale lowing outside, this was a warm and cozy nook with its tender sunset light, the fragrance of burning blubber and mellowing meats, and such a fearless hunter as Ernenek snoring in the bag.

But Asiak yearned for the sun's summoning, when they could drive southward to meet the herds, and life would consist of excitement that might help her forget; of stalking the caribou and musk ox and setting snares and traps, and perhaps meeting large crowds of other men, possibly as many as eight or ten people, and with them hunt and make merry.

In her heart, hope for Papik's recovery had been short-lived and she regretted having taken him back.

Separation would be unbearable now.

Spring came, the long dawn, the slow aurora, paling the stars, turning purple, turning light, turning day, and at long last—the sun! And Asiak, after time-honored custom, extinguished the light, poured out the fuel, and rekindled the lamp with fresh blubber and a new wick.

And in stride with the breath of life reappearing from below the horizon, drowsiness dropped from the Men, their wasted bodies clamored for flesh and the blood pulsed faster through their veins, making them restless, causing them to inspect and reinspect the lashings of their sleds and whet the tips of spears and arrows and tighten the sinews that spanned their bows.

His muscular body glistening with grease, Ernenek stood amid the glowing ice walls. "At our first stop we'll abandon the two."

"But somebody has grown very fond of Papik," said Asiak, feeling her heart turn colder than an abandoned igloo. "Even as he grows bigger a silly mother could chew his food in her own mouth."

"And what when you die? The men will mock and the women scorn him, all his life. No, no. He is not fit to live." And he turned round and went to harness the huskies, muttering.

When the sled was packed and the huskies were barking impatiently, Powtee emerged from the igloo with Papik in her arms.

"You can take him along without me. It came to pass that his teeth have started to grow."

There they were, under Asiak's probing finger, two sharp,

tiny chips of tooth, and Powtee promised that more would be forthcoming, a whole row of them, a full and straight and white team of them. How she had done it, what she had done, nobody knows. But the story is true, because Ittimangnerk, the trader, who saw Ernenek's family the following summer and bartered tea for some of their foxskins, told it to somebody who had never caught him lying, except for business reasons.

Asiak fell upon her mother's neck and snuffed at her walnut-stained face and rubbed her nose against it and washed it with tears, and Ernenek bounced higher than a young seal showing off before his first bride, and making very similar sounds.

"You must stay with us, little one," Asiak told Powtee. "What if our next children are born without teeth?"

"Do not worry. The Powers of the Winds and Snows have promised that all your children shall be provided with teeth, even if they don't show any at first. Some old woman is weary of these long journeys. She feels drowsy and wayworn and weak. The spring no longer stirs her blood."

Departure at this point being improper they opened a bundle and returned indoors to brew some tea and prattle and catch up on laughter and pull at Papik's teeth and drop tidbits into his mouth, and once Asiak had to reach deep into his throat where too big a morsel had got stuck. They gorged and guzzled and made merry till Asiak, who had slept little this winter, was overcome by sudden weariness and lay down to rest. Ernenek kept stuffing his face with meat and cracking bones for the marrow till he also grew sleepy and went down snoring.

Powtee rose and quietly slipped out. The team barked at her but she shushed them, clouting the more demonstrative ones vigorously over the head with the handle of her snow knife. She had left behind her inner suit of aukskins that might come in handy to Asiak or the little one, for it took a lot of sewing to fit so many small skins together, and wore her seediest dogskin garments with scarcely any hair left on them.

A rousing gale greeted her bluffly under a sulky sky. Progress was laborious to her leathered old body that had burned high energy all winter with barely any refueling. There was no sound but the crunch of her pads on the harsh snow, and way underfoot the muffled rumble of the sea, of the warm sea, the good rich sea filled with the good, fat fish.

She pressed on till she broke into a sweat, which she had been trained to avoid carefully since earliest childhood unless she was in her sleeping bag. But she kept on trudging with all her waning might, straining and perspiring. On an ice ridge in mid-sea she stopped. The igloo was no longer visible to her life-weary eyes.

She sat down and waited placidly for the sweat on her body to turn to ice.

Time passed. She didn't know how long, nor did anyone know or care, nor did it matter.

At first the frost about her body was painful. She felt the cast of ice chill her flesh, and bones, and thoughts. Sensation waned and departed, the mind grew sluggish in line with the slowing blood, and sweet drowsiness came. Before long she no longer felt cold, but cozy and contented.

She made out the shape of a bear jogging over the sea fields and thought of Ernenek's joy if he were to sight the great beast. It was approaching warily, restraining its nine hundred pounds of hunger, diffident of anything that had semblance of man, because man had so much the semblance of bear. It moved over the ice with a ponderousness that was only apparent, its small ears alert, its broad mobile nose and pin-point eyes alive in its jolly triangular face, making low, gurgling sounds and puffs of respiration in the cold.

Powtee couldn't help but grin a little with her toothless mouth about the fact that the mere human shape was sufficient to keep at bay so big a beast. And she reflected that the bear was right in being wary, for surely someday Ernenek would meet it face to face on the white sea, inveigle it into swallowing a ball of spring bait and follow it in its sickness till he could slay it. Before a new igloo the old shouts of joy would rise as the hunter skinned the kill and his mate removed the entrails before they froze and their son bit into the fuming liver with his row of perfect ivory teeth, till of the big white hunter nothing would be left but the blood stains on the wall.

Powtee knew the future because she knew the past, and her familiarity with the facts of life allowed her to understand, and therefore accept without bitterness, nature's eternal tragedy—that flesh must perish so that flesh may live. She was to die so that the bear might live for the day when Ernenek could slay it to feed Asiak and Papik.

And so she would return to them.

By the time the bear closed in, almost all feeling had left her, and it was with hardly any pain at all that she passed on to the regions of the constant and unruffled slumber.

CHAPTER FOUR

The Bargain

WHILE among the evergreens the Polar Eskimos pined and died, they thrived on the perennial ice. In winter they erected their five-foot igloos on the ocean's petrified crust which, due to the underlying waters, was warmer than the land. In springtime they emerged from their dark torpor, shed their clothes, scraped the grime from their bodies and ate it, mated promiscuously, exchanging their partners, sang and danced to the surging day, fished in the ice holes, speared the ringed seal and chased the white bear, unless they traveled to the southward to meet the herds and glean precious driftwood from the liquefied ocean.

The procurement of food was their main endeavor. And since wherever people appeared game soon became scarce, they were forced to avoid human company, constantly changing their hunting grounds, perpetually on the move. When they cached away meat stores that came in handy in times of dearth it was not out of concern for tomorrow, but because they could neither consume nor carry it all and were impatient to move on. They didn't worry about the future any more than about the past, but thought only of the everlasting present.

While most other tribes had been touched and tainted by civilization, the scattering of Polar Eskimos, who confined their nomad existence to the Central Arctic near the Magnetic Pole, a region too remote and forbidding for white men to reach, had not changed their crude mode of living since the world was young. They were like children, forthright, pitiless, and gay. In the age of tanks they still hunted with bow and stone-tipped arrows, shared the fruit of their hunt, and were too artless to lie. So crude were they.

Ernenek and Asiak might have lived on in this way indefinitely had not Ittimangnerk, the traveling salesman, planted the seed of curiosity into their hearts.

Ittimangnerk was a hybrid and a mongrel—half native and half alien, half hunter and half trader, half fish and half fowl. Circumstance had cast him early in life into the path of white men, infecting him with their passions and everlasting strife, without quite killing the Eskimo in him; condemning him to waver forever between the two, happy nowhere, loved by no one.

Fall had already scattered the watery sunlight of summer, tainting the Glacial Ocean a graying mauve, when Ittimangnerk and his wife, Hiko, spotted Ernenek's igloo glowing faintly in the evening dusk.

Ernenek, stripped down to his socks and gleaming with grease, was at play with that unbreakable toy that was little Papik, pulling him around on the ground among the gnawed fish heads and bones. He loudly welcomed the visitors, shaking their hands and poking Ittimangnerk's stomach to see how he was faring, while Asiak dropped her housework to make tea. She broke off some drinking snow and put it over the lamp, for whatever they drank had first to be melted. Then she took the guests' outer suits and boots off and inspected them for rips to mend.

But there was nothing to mend: the newly arrived had obviously stopped a little way off and changed into a fresh suit of clothes before entering the igloo, as their garments were dry and bore none of the unmistakable marks of the trail. Hiko was a sight. While her husband was dressed almost like a regular man, she wore soft boots of reindeer cow trimmed with ermine tails, a jacket of flimsy fox fur, and colored beads and ribbons in her hair the like Asiak had never seen and which intrigued her greatly.

Ittimangnerk wasted no time in proving that, if not his clothes, his manners were outlandish. He didn't invite his hosts to rummage in his bundles and pillage them, as custom demanded, nor did he forthwith attack their larder, as tradition permitted. He was shockingly jealous of his possessions and refused to accept gifts in order not to feel indebted. But he was always disposed to swap, a process he had learned from the white men.

He had no leisure for social amenities and couldn't afford to laugh and eat for a fortnight before coming to the point of his visit. So after only a few hours of sipping cool tea, sucking at some of his own frozen fish, telling the latest bawdy gossip amid uproarious laughter, and a little nap, he displayed his wares: black tea leaves packed in the dried bladder of a reindeer cow, and a coil of wick.

"Have you any foxskins?" he asked, glancing about.

"Maybe there are some behind the lamp," Ernenek said. "Take all you want."

Ittimangnerk examined the skins. "Somebody can use only these seven. In exchange you get one package of tea and four arm lengths of wick. It is a new kind of wick, made of tundra cotton, which gives a brighter flame and lasts longer than the usual moss. If you kept the skins neat, without using them for mops, somebody would give you more tea and more wick."

At this, Ernenek split his sides with laughter. When he was able to speak he said, "But somebody doesn't *want* more tea or wick!"

"Wait, and you will see something you will want," Ittimangnerk said. He plunged into the tunnel and returned at once with an oblong package. He took off the skin wrapping and out came a gun. It was a Martini military rifle of venerable vintage, but it might have been the latest model so far as Ernenek was concerned, who had never heard of firearms.

"Do you eat it?" asked Asiak.

"This is a shotgun, the white man's weapon," Ittimangnerk said importantly. "Even a child can kill a big bear with it, and you don't have to make him sick first and then chase him till he is ready to be killed. You just touch this lever and the bear goes flat on his back without arguing."

And since Ittimangnerk's familiarity with firearms was only slightly greater than Ernenek's, he leaned somewhat too heavily on the trigger and the thing went off, darkening the tiny abode with smoke and shaking the air.

For a moment they all looked at each other, thunderstruck, and Papik started to cry. Then Ittimangnerk, caught by the sudden frenzy of the Men, fired again and again, and the igloo grew darker and darker, and the bullets whizzed round the circular wall, chipping the ice, until the magazine was empty.

When the smoke had cleared somewhat through the opening in the roof Ernenek, bewildered, showed a small hole in his buttock where a ricocheting bullet had lodged.

Now it was Ittimangnerk who had a fit of merriment. He sagged on the couch, holding his belly, Hiko dutifully echoing his merriment, and Ernenek grinned back half-heartedly.

But Asiak couldn't see the joke. With her little finger she probed the wound, extracted the bullet with the point of her snow knife and stopped the hole, which had begun bleeding more freely, with fish-liver oil that the cold had hardened to a paste.

Ernenek's big face showed no emotion throughout the operation. When it was over he grinned, but Asiak glowered at Ittimangnerk.

"Somebody only wanted to demonstrate how it works," Ittimangnerk said apologetically. "How could one know the bullet would jump back? It shows you the gun's power. It slays any animal from a distance, if you don't hit a wall first."

Ernenek took the rifle into his hands and Asiak hastened to throw her arms round Papik.

"Don't fear," Ittimangnerk said. "The bullets are finished and new ones can be had at the trading post only."

"What do you want for this?" Ernenek asked, peering into the barrel.

"Many more foxskins than you now have. But once you have gathered enough and go to the trading post, mentioning my name, the white man will give you one."

"How many skins are needed?"

"Five times a man counted to the end."

Ernenek pondered the answer with knitted brow, and shuddered. Finger and toe enumeration being the only method of counting, a-man-counted-to-the-end meant twenty, the highest known figure. Five men counted to the

end was more than Ernenek could visualize. But he realized it meant a lot.

"Somebody could also bring musk ox and caribou
hides," he said hopefully.

"The white man wants foxskins only. His likings are
queer but he knows what he wants. His brain isn't very
sharp but his head is very hard."

Ernenek and Asiak wanted to hear more about the white
man and his oddness, and while bending their ears they
distributed slabs of mellow seal which, business having
been concluded, were now accepted. Everybody gnawed
and gulped and belched between tales and questions, and
every once in a while Asiak put her lips against Papik's and
blew into his mouth masticated meat that the little one
munched messily, bespattering his chin with gore.

Ernenek did a lot of laughing with Hiko and so did
Asiak with Ittimangnerk. Small wonder the lonesome couple of the North wanted their guests to stay on and bright-
en the monotony of the Polar night, but Ittimangnerk was
a busy man and after a forty-eight-hour nap he left with
Hiko, showing for once that he could be well mannered
if he chose to: by sneaking out tactfully while his hosts
were napping, and taking along the ripest bear ham in the
house—probably in an effort to show his admiration for
the greater hunter Ernenek.

The plant of curiosity took root and grew on and on.

Although in a winter igloo there was plenty to do between sleeps—for Ernenek to fashion utensils, whet weapons and repair harnesses, for Asiak to sew garments and
feed little Papik who sucked even in his slumber—yet the
siren call of adventure and worlds to discover made the
couple restless.

Ernenek raved about the gun's magnificent noise, Asiak
wondered no end about life at the trading post about which

Hiko and Ittimangnerk had aroused her curiosity without satisfying it.

"The white man," she would say musingly, "has no liking for frozen fish and rotted meat. He spoils all food by holding it over the fire."

"But he has many guns," Ernenek would rise to his white brother's defense, "and you wouldn't be able to imitate their boom even if you tried."

"He lives in an enormous house of wood, sticky with heat, and suffers from cold all the time."

"But he has more bullets than you have wits and each bullet can fell a bear, like that. He must eat bear liver and bear tongue all his life."

When day and spring and life returned to the top of the world Ernenek did not saw fish holes in the ice, nor listen at the seals' blowholes, nor drive south to meet the herds that pastured on the lichen beneath the snow, and even the distant sight of bear slinking over the sea fields or waltzing down an iceberg caused no stir in him. If he abandoned the Glacial Ocean and went to live inland in a tent of skins it was only to do what he had heretofore considered woman's work: setting snares and digging pitfalls among the dwarf vegetation that was laboriously crawling out from under the wintry crust—snares made of sinew and wood and bone, snares with springs and trapdoors and nooses; steep pitfalls baited with blubber or meat; and when he sighted a fox on the loose he waddled after it, shooting his stone-tipped arrows.

Asiak, meanwhile, rode to the far-flung caches to draw from the stored provisions, collected whatever leaves could be brewed for tea, looked for iron pyrites, or garnered fungi which, dried in the sun, provided touchwood.

In summer, while hunting or servicing the traps, they dispensed almost entirely with sleep, but fed stupendously, and this year more than ever—Ernenek because he went after fox unsparingly; Asiak because she was pregnant;

Papik because he was growing; and the dogs for no good reason at all. And although they ate every scrap of the skinned foxes the provisions dwindled swiftly and Asiak began to worry.

"When winter comes there won't be much to go on."

"Then one will eat a little less," Ernenek answered blithely, as if he would be the one to tighten his belt. "But once we have a gun it will be so easy to kill game that you can become twice as fat as now."

Garnering so many foxes was no laughing matter. There was plenty of easier game, seal and walrus and, only about a year farther south, musk ox and caribou. But no animal was foxier than a fox in avoiding capture—except, of course, a wolverine.

Sometimes the caught fox escaped, leaving a leg behind. Sometimes a whole row of snares had been sprung, out of sheer devilry, by the mad and maddening wolverine that had escaped unharmed, not without retrieving the bait; and when a fox had been trapped the wolverine had playfully torn it to tatters, or carried it off along with the trap.

If Ernenek could but once lay hands on a live wolverine! And he had seldom ever caught sight of one of those impudent, sanguinary little beasts, invisible except in motion, too clever to budge when people were around, and apparently busy all day doing things that had no reward but the vexation of man.

Yet by constantly changing his trapping grounds, setting snares faster than the wolverine could spring them and making the circuit of traps before the foxes might chew through their own legs or the wolverine ravage them, he caught the required number. By then he had his fill of their sweet and stringy meat, had depleted the caches and all but cleaned out the larder. But he could wave the skins before Asiak's nose whenever, in feminine alarmism, she prophesied starvation and the inevitable extinction of little Papik, followed by her own, and finally that of Ernenek, alone, forsaken and remorse-bitten.

By then the sun had spiraled below the horizon on its six-months' vacation and the first stars were beginning to break through the tightening veil of the evening. Ernenek wanted to start for the trading post without delay. But here Asiak opposed him determinedly.

"First we must sleep a few months, for somebody is becoming drowsy after a very tiresome summer," she said.

"If we leave in a few months we won't reach the trading post before the great thaw sets in. The sea there melts every year. The time for traveling south is now."

"If the sea melts we'll wait on land till it freezes again. It always does, you know."

"Yes, but we'll waste time."

"We have time to waste."

"But somebody doesn't like wasting time!" Ernenek said virtuously.

But Asiak remained adamant, and Ernenek knew of no way he could change a woman's mind outside a sleeping bag. So he went fishing and sealing in the gloom of fall, listlessly, all the while looking with scorn and ill humor upon his bow and spear.

When winter had grown dark, driving some of the game to the southward and some under cover and forcing even Ernenek to don his second suit of bearhide and double the layer of fish grease on his face against the bite of frost, they abandoned the forbidding land and drove out to sea where they built their tiny igloo over the warmth of the water. This was the time for rest and quiet housework, and Asiak hoped Ernenek would sleep off his energy.

But he kept mumbling nervously about the gun in fitful slumber.

In the dead of night Asiak suddenly said:

"Going on like this is a waste of time. A woman can

barely sleep nor does she have her mind on her work. Maybe things will be settled by driving to the trading post. Ittimangnerk said it is only a couple of moons away, traveling fast."

Swift as an accident Ernenek was on his soles, checking traces and lashings and hastening outside to dig out the sled and prepare the runners, while Asiak packed the household utensils and provisions into skins, leaving nothing behind but the food scraps on the floor.

The dogs, once their drowsiness was gone, began battling one another and their leader had to charge them to bring them in line. Ernenek slaughtered the four smallest puppies and chopped them up to carry along as feed for the team.

Ittimangnerk couldn't have described the route more clearly:

"You cross the Bay of the One-Eyed Seal, drive between the two pointed islands known as Devil's Fangs, follow the land to your left, pass the narrow strait called Beartongue Channel, then follow the low coastline to the right. Stay away from that shore, as the Inland People would most probably kill and eat you if you landed, but keep driving on the ocean till you come to a long range of bluffs. There keep your eyes peeled for the river openings. The trading post is up the fourth river, at the second bend, right on the bank. You can't miss it."

They couldn't miss it, nor could anything untoward happen to them on the way, for they were abundantly insured against the thwackings of fate: they carried a tuft of white rabbit hair against frostbite, and ermine's tail against blizzards, a bear's claw against lightning, a caribou's tooth against famine, a lemming's skin against disease, a wolverine's paw against madness, a fox head against trickery, a dried guillemot for luck in fishing, a reindeer's ear for fine hearing, a louse for invisibility to enemies as lice are masters at concealment, a batch of soot for endurance because soot outlasts fire, and a seal's eye against the evil eye and various hostile spirits. Even the dogs wore amulets. Small wonder they proceeded swiftly and unhindered before a following wind—the north wind, that all winter hardly ever relented.

As the team fined down, their speed increased. The cold, for all its sharpness, failed to cut through the riders' double clothing and the double coat the huskies had started growing in fall, but it hardened the blubber on the riders' faces to a crust, their breath frosted their nostrils and eyelashes, and when they spat, the spittle froze in mid-air and clicked on the ground. Papik, strapped to his mother's back inside her trundle hood, experienced nothing but the warmth of her body.

Whenever they noticed the frost creeping into their flesh they jumped off the sled and ran alongside until they were warm. They took naps on the ride, but when the team showed signs of fatigue, Ernenek flung the sled anchor overboard and called a halt.

He used the stop to re-ice the runners or to fish. As it was impossible to carry enough provisions for so many mouths on so long a trip it was necessary to spear food from the ocean. This was not easy in winter. Only near promontories and around icebergs could stretches be found where the freeze was not too thick to be pierced, and then it took a lot of poring over the hole and a lot of moonlight before Ernenek retrieved some sun-colored salmon or blood-red trout.

As soon as a halt was called the dogs dropped in their tracks. Since there was not enough snow on the ground to burrow themselves in for warmth they huddled together, coiled into round balls of fur with their noses behind their paws and their backs to the wind. Soon they were nothing but one motionless heap and it took many kicks and blows to make them seem alive again. Perpetually famished, they could devour daily their own weight in flesh, spreading like bloated bladders, but were trained to forego food for three or four days when on the trail, for ten when out of work. Since they never got their fill they didn't grow lazy and trotted all the way with their tails in the air.

On the trail they were always full of life and pranks. When their masters had walked away leaving the sled unanchored, the head dog might bark the signal of departure and the whole team would tear away for all they were worth, and Ernenek and Asiak nearly broke their necks to catch up with them.

Most of the time the sky was cloudless and they rode under a glittering canopy in which the North star blazed central and supreme, and the wind was fragrant with the scent of ozone. When the moon rose, it remained above the horizon for more than a week at a time. The ghostly coastline, which they never let out of sight, was then sharply emblazoned against the brilliant sky, and the icebergs, the islands and ridges cast deep-blue shadows on the pearly landscape.

Sometimes they could hear the ice crack in its perpetual, uneasy movement; then they would strain for sound and sight, ready to curb the team. Most gaps could be jumped by the huskies and bridged by the sled, but once they met a crevasse which was too wide. It had just formed, for the water could still be heard beating against the sheer ice walls ten or twelve feet below and pressing to the surface, and they had to skirt it for a long stretch before resuming their course. In some places the ice crust had buckled under the pressure of submarine currents into great ridges in which a passageway had to be found, making advance as difficult as over land.

When one of the rare winter blizzards rose howling, filling the air with blinding ice dust and sweeping the roof of the world clear of all that moved and much that didn't, they halted and hastily built a shelter, Ernenek cutting the blocks and heaving them in place, Asiak packing the chinks from outside, till the little shelter stood safely encrusted in the ice, barely showing above the surface of the ocean—shield against the weather, shell designed to retain the warmth of the human body.

Inside, they gnawed at some frozen fish and munched a little snow, crept into their bags, and were lulled to sleep by the sound of the storm raging overhead and the ocean rumbling underfoot. Asiak was always the first to wake in the gray mist that had formed after the lamp had gone out. First she scratched off the rime of frozen breath that crusted her face. Then, without leaving the couch, she brewed tea, took the dried clothes and boots from the rack and started softening them with scraper and teeth.

Before the tea froze she woke Ernenek.

The snow on the ground increased as they moved southward, bothering the dogs who had no way of protecting their faces from it, and shortly before reaching the trading post it grew so warm that Ernenek stripped to the waist and rode bare-chested in the unbearable heat of some fifteen below.

They stopped in awe to behold the white man's post from a distance before entering it. Ittimangnerk had not exaggerated. Its size! Its shape! What beauty! What luxury!

It was a one-room cabin of smoke-blackened logs with two sooty windows hung with icicles. Along the walls were two double lines of ship bunks, one above the other, and there was a counter, several cases and shelves, a frame partition, a stove and, as if that weren't enough, a table and several chairs, all made of wood, the rarest and most valuable of materials, and everything glaringly illuminated by a kerosene lamp.

And the number of people crowding the place! Exactly a man counted to the end—an even twenty, as Asiak established after elaborate reckoning, which didn't include the children in the women's trundle hoods. And their speech! Fascinating, because often impossible to understand, sprinkled as it was with alien words. Many men grinned at her admiringly and she giggled back embarrassed.

Then the white man came out from behind the partition.

He was odd on many counts: his bearing, his gait, his huge hands, his impractical clothes and, more than anything else, the red beard hanging from his narrow, unsmiling face. The natives were in the habit of plucking what scanty hair grew on their chins in order to prevent the accumulation of frost, and but few raised reluctant mustaches.

"Somebody expected him to be white as snow," Asiak whispered disappointed, "after all that talk of the white man. He is darker than we are if we scrape the soot from our faces."

"It has come to pass," Ernenek addressed the white man, ignoring a woman's chatter and getting down to business, "that somebody, sent by Ittimangnerk, has brought with him a few foxskins." And he waited hopefully.

But the white man showed no sign of understanding. He called, "Undik!" and a gray-haired Eskimo with a face as craggy as a glacier and a walrus mustache that hung perpendicularly down his chin, approached, rolling like a bear on his bowlegs. He wore native boots and trousers but an outlandish leather jacket over a checkered woolen shirt.

"What brings you here?" he inquired. "The white man doesn't speak the language of the Men."

Ernenek and Asiak exchanged a glance and burst into roars of laughter. After a little of this the white man stamped his foot and Undik said impatiently:

"What do you want? It seems you mentioned Ittimangnerk."

Ernenek repressed his laughter and stated the reason for his visit.

"Get your skins," Undik said. "He will look at them."

Everyone crowded close as Ernenek opened his bundles and spread the bloody skins on the floor. The white man inspected them one by one with a frown on his face. At the end he spoke to Undik, gravely.

"He says they aren't quite what he wanted," Undik translated, "but he will let you have a gun anyway." He went behind the partition and returned with an ancient gun, the grandfather of the one Ittimangnerk had so efficaciously demonstrated in the igloo, and handed it to Ernenek.

"If you want bullets you must bring more skins. There is one bullet in the gun to show that it works. But you must take it outside."

From the doorway Ernenek fired away into the night and turned around beaming. "It makes even more noise than the other," he said to Asiak, while the wind blew in the smoke of the gunpowder. Then he turned to Undik:

"Tell the white man that if he wishes to laugh with somebody's wife he is welcome to her." He looked at Asiak, who blushed and giggled.

"No, no," Undik said. "He doesn't like to laugh with the women of the Men, nor does he allow anyone else to laugh in his presence. So take heed."

Ernenek and Asiak looked flustered and mortified, and Undik added soothingly, "You may rest here if you are tired."

They were tired but didn't feel like resting. Too many odd things went on in this fabulous house and they couldn't miss a single one. Little Papik also was all eyes and ears, but he was shy and clung to his mother's trousers.

The people in this place ate strange foods coming out of tin cans and heated on the stove, and drank their tea steaming hot. Not only their ways of eating and drinking, but everything they had and did and said was intriguing. They had knives of gleaming metal that cut meat like blubber, and the advantage of this was obvious; but the games of cards they played and all the items and habits they had acquired from white man remained mysterious, although everybody vied with each other to illuminate the unsophisticated couple from the North, just as they went to great lengths to explain the principles of trade, what a sale and a barter and a bargain was.

Some were drinking a brown liquid from glass bottles and since it was the first time Ernenek saw glass he touched a bottle, and its owner grinned and asked, "Do you want to taste it?"

If Ernenek had taken but a sip, and not right away a big swill, it might have hit him less hard; but then he wouldn't have been Ernenek. He could swallow fishbones without harm, but the draught from that bottle shot like a spear thrust down his throat. He choked and coughed and spat, his face turned crimson and his eyes watered, while the cabin rocked with laughter. When it was over he thought a joke had been played on him and tried to laugh it off, though he considered it a most clumsy joke.

"You will get accustomed to it," said the owner of the bottle. "It is called firewater. It doesn't taste good but keeps you warm."

"Somebody is too warm already," Ernenek snorted, beginning to get rid of his clothes. But here Undik put a restraining hand on his shoulder:

"The white man doesn't approve of naked people."

Ernenek looked round in astonishment. It hadn't occurred to him before, but actually everybody was fully dressed although the place was stifling with heat.

Winter was the season for traveling and visiting in the South, where the big thaw restricted summer journeys, and the hunters and trappers and their wives wanted to make the most of their presence at the trading post. Chatting, eating and drinking went on for a while, until the white man retired behind his partition and Undik announced it was time to turn out the light.

Ernenek and Asiak were invited to try the bunks. Asiak accepted but Ernenek, chary of new practical jokes, thought it safer to stretch out on the floor, beside other men left without bunks. The chinks of the blazing stove were the only things visible in the dark. Some men kept on talking shop for a while before joining the chorus of snorers.

Outside, the north wind howled and the cabin creaked in its structure.

Asiak was wide awake. The air was stuffy with heat and the unfamiliar odors of kerosene, coal, tobacco and cooked foods, and she was dizzy with the kaleidoscope of experiences. She pressed Papik to her bosom and snuffed at him, feeling alien in an alien world.

"Ernenek," she called. "Are you awake?"

"Yes," Ernenek answered from the floor.

"There is something wrong."

"What?"

"Something is wrong with the white man. Why doesn't he know that a small igloo is quicker to build and easier to keep warm than so huge a house? He must walk to what he needs, instead of just reaching out for it, and sometimes he doesn't find what he is looking for despite the glaring light. He may have a lot of guns but somebody doubts if they are any good for killing game, or why would he eat those ill-smelling things out of iron boxes? And why does he drink firewater that burns your throat? And why doesn't he allow taking off one's clothes when it is too warm? And why does he never smile? And why doesn't he laugh with the women of the Men, and objects even to other people laughing?"

"What do you mean by all that talk?" Ernenek said irritably, to show his authority. "A woman making noise!"

"Yes, excuse a silly woman for speaking before so many men, but she thinks that if the white man is stupid one shouldn't accept all those gifts from him, and if he is crazy one shouldn't have anything to do with him, because craziness is catching. It seems advisable to leave this place and never come back."

"But it will be necessary to come back to bring the skins to get the bullets!"

By now all snoring had ceased and everyone was listening in with great delight.

"Well then," Asiak said in sudden resolution, climbing out of her bunk. "You can get your bullets, and a woman will get a new husband."

She stumbled over the furniture in the dark and stepped on someone's nose. That couldn't happen in an igloo, she thought, trying to locate her outer suit. She found it, not without difficulty, donned it, and opened the door letting in an icy squall.

"A worthless woman is looking for a new man," she announced to the room. "A woman stupid and ugly and old, but sometimes lucky at skinning game and tanning hides and sewing with small stitches and making fine needles, and at doing other little things to make a man feel comfortable. But he must be a good provider, for the woman in question has one child on her back and one in her belly." This said, she turned round and waddled off into the night.

A soapstone lamp, given by Ernenek to Asiak's parents, had been sufficient to seal their marriage; and a soapstone lamp on her husband's head might be enough to break it— meaning the head, the lamp, or the marriage.

The sky was overcast and she had difficulty in finding the team among the many huddled in the snow. Bending against the gale and swaying to its gusts she began setting up the sled.

From the cabin a man came up to her in the dark.

"Somebody can do with a woman," he shouted against the wind. "Since my own disappeared in an icebreak last winter I found out a woman is as necessary as a team of huskies. I don't care if I never come back to the trading post."

"Are you a good hunter?" asked Asiak, trying to pierce the night. His outline wasn't much to look at. "Have you still all your teeth?"

The stranger chuckled. "Such a good hunter am I that I not only have a gun," and he flaunted it before Asiak's nose, "but also enough bullets for a lifetime. And I have all my teeth except two."

Someone else was approaching. Asiak recognized Ernenek's swagger and bulky frame, and answered raising her voice:

"I'll come with you if you hurry."

Ernenek had reached them. "Go away," he growled at the stranger, who growled back:

"You heard the woman. Out of my way, man!"

Ernenek had been unable to find his snow knife in the dark cabin and was unarmed, so he closed in with his fists. The stranger chuckled. He couched his gun like a spear, put the barrel against Ernenek's chest and fired away.

Most of that weapon's value lay in the smoke screen it made. After the gale had cleared it Asiak saw Ernenek sprawling in the snow and the stranger doubled over from the gun's kickback, pressing his stomach.

The lust of anger pervaded her. She snatched up the gun which the man had dropped and smashed it over his head again and again. The gun broke first, the stock flying away in pieces, and the stranger trotted off, whimpering.

Then she knelt down by Ernenek.

A shaft of light came from the cabin and all the teams,

aroused by the shot, barked, howled and whined. The white man, followed by the Eskimos, hurried cursing to the scene, carrying a hurricane lamp that jolted as he ran. The shot had burned a hole in Ernenek's jacket and the bullet stuck deep in his collarbone. This time he winced and groaned as Asiak probed the wound with the point of her snow knife.

"Since you are able to move your arm we can leave the bullet in. At least," she added, "from now on you can always say you have a bullet."

Ernenek stood up, a trifle shaky and grinning sheepishly.

"Let us leave," said Asiak. "Please get his outer suit."

"This is Ernenek," Ernenek said, "and not the man you want to leave with."

Asiak shrugged. "The other ran away, and one is as bad as the next."

There were cheers and grins and guffaws from the circle of onlookers at the sight of the small family perched on top of the bundles. Even the white man couldn't help smiling, and Undik slapped Ernenek's shoulder, saying, "Go back where you belong, man, and stay there." Then he and the others turned away.

The huskies pulled off and the sled started with a jerk that made the riders sway. But they had not gone far when Ernenek called a halt.

"It came to pass that somebody forgot his gun," he said, scratching his head.

"A clumsy woman broke the stranger's gun over his head, so she told Undik to give him yours. But if we must eat foxmeat again for a whole summer in order to get another gun, then you better get it back right now."

Ernenek pondered over it, then shook his head. "The gun is no good. One can't kill anything with it."

"A stupid woman knew that all the time. Now let us put

some distance between us and the trading post, then stop and build an igloo. We haven't slept a week all winter."

"We got rid of our foxskins and didn't get the gun—what a great trade that was!" jeered Ernenek.

"It was a bargain," Asiak said thoughtfully.

Ernenek shouted and cracked his whip and the dogs barked and strained, spreading fanwise, panting and yapping, blowing nervous plumes of steam from their noses.

CHAPTER FIVE

White Man in the White Land

THEIR contact with the white man had been so fleeting that sometimes Ernenek and Asiak doubted whether it had taken place anywhere except in their imaginations. But they didn't worry about it unduly. Not yet. Ernenek was busy with the hunt and Asiak with family matters.

Remembering that breast feeding, by inhibiting menstruation, might keep a woman barren for a long time after childbearing, Asiak would have suckled her son for many years to come, as all the women she had met did, for the life they led made pregnancy uncomfortable and prevented the raising of large families. But before Papik was three years old Asiak was compelled to wean him, as in his craving of meat he kept wounding her with his sharp little teeth.

Shortly after the visit to the trading post Asiak brought forth a girl that she named Ivaloo. By this time Papik had done considerable growing, had become broad and strong, a real little Man, who showed promise of turning into a valiant hunter someday. And how could it be otherwise with one who carried his dried navel string sewn inside his clothes? Who with his first teeth had been made to eat a dog's head so that his own head might grow wise and

strong? Who on his wrist carried the penis of a r
which insured his future ability as a sealer, while t   scraps
of bearskin in his pants guaranteed his growing into a
valiant bear hunter?

And Papik was going to need all the charms he could get
now that a new hazard was increasing the natural dangers
of the North.

The new hazard was called white man.

When Ivaloo was two a group of explorers penetrated
so far north beyond the Arctic Circle that they touched
the southernmost hunting line of the Polar Eskimos. Ernenek and Asiak spotted their camp in spring and could not
resist the temptation to visit it.

The expedition consisted of eight white men and more
Eskimos than a man counted to the end. Also staggering
was the number of their sleds and dogs: nineteen sleds and
numberless dogs—far more than Ernenek or Asiak could
count.

The Eskimos came from distant southern tribes who also
called themselves Men, though Ernenek didn't. They
seemed as crazy as wolverines, eating the white men's
foods, aping the white men's habits. The white men believed those Eskimos could guide them over great distances
in the frozen land, but Ernenek knew better. According to
him, the southern Eskimos didn't know a lot more than
white man, which wasn't much, and sometimes they knew
less.

When Ernenek began to rummage in the explorers'
cases one of them struck his fingers with a stick, which sent
him brooding in a corner. When later on they offered him
some firewater he knew they were decidedly hostile and he
made up his mind to leave.

It would have been better if he had. But Asiak was
tired, the weather was forbidding, and they decided to
build an igloo and go down for a nap.

Asiak woke up Ernenek with a joyful announcement: "We have a guest!"

One of the white men, an ill-nourished, lemming-faced little fellow with drooping shoulders had just crawled in and was beating the snow from his clothes. The cold had turned his face blue and his nose red and laden his large flap-ears with chilblains. Ernenek, feeling honored, beamed and grinned at him.

The visitor squatted on the couch and gazed about with evident curiosity. But when he discovered that he had landed in the droppings of the puppies he looked very annoyed. Asiak wiped him with a foxskin, laughing, and said, "It's only filth." Yet he fastidiously picked a clean spot before sitting down again, then pulled out a pad and pencil and began to scribble while the children gaped at him goggle-eyed. From time to time he picked up a household implement, turned it over in his hands and drew lines on his pad. Ernenek and Asiak peeked over his shoulder. He was making quite accurate drawings of the igloo and its contents. But the pained expression never left his face.

When Ernenek pushed under his nose a lump of moldering liver he didn't, as any well-bred man would have done, click his tongue and smack his lips, but jerked his head away as if it were refuse; and his face wrinkled up into a grimace of disgust at Ernenek's next offer: a beautiful piece of marrow more than a year old, swarming with maggots.

Ernenek's good humor was vanishing.

"Did the white man come to insult us?" he asked Asiak.

"Maybe he is used to different foods."

"Maybe he left his manners behind."

"Now remember that he is our guest, so don't be a bear and break some of his bones," Asiak cautioned. "We would lose a lot of face if you did."

Ernenek made a last attempt with a savory delicacy he had reserved for himself—a thoroughly chewed hodgepodge of caribou eyes, ptarmigan dung, auk slime and fermented bear brain, but all to no avail.

"Why did he come into our igloo if he doesn't appreciate our foods?" he cried while the blood rushed to his face.

"Maybe he is not hungry. Maybe he just wants to laugh with a worthless woman."

"Remember the white man at the trading post? He didn't want to."

"Some do, some don't. I have made inquiries among other women and it seems that some white men are very fond of laughing with the women of the Men. They even give them beautiful presents afterward. Also to their husbands."

"Maybe that's what he wants," Ernenek said, beaming again all over. "Make yourself beautiful."

Tittering, Asiak let her hair down, rolled up her sleeves and dunked her arms into the urine tub, passing her fingers through her hair till it was smooth and shiny. Mirroring herself in the tub, with the spine of a fish she combed her hair and rearranged it. Then she scooped up a handful of blubber from the lamp, where it was near-melted from the flame, rubbed it into her face, and sat down on the couch beside the white man who had followed her antics with a puzzled eye. He backed up with a face of fright and she moved up to him, offering her grin and blushing.

"Don't be embarrassed," Ernenek smirked at him. "A husband is taking the children for a little walk." Then, remembering that the guest didn't know the language of the Men, he signaled with his hands that he was leaving.

At this the white man flung himself to the ground and tried to run the gauntlet. But Ernenek, eyes blazing, grabbed him by the seat of his pants as he wiggled through the tunnel and tossed him back onto the couch while Asiak, utterly mortified, burst into tears.

"Son of a tailless bitch and a toothless walrus!" Ernenek

thundered at his cringing guest. "How dare you so insult a man?" He picked him up again and dashed him repeatedly against the wall, till the explorer's head grew limp and his skull made a dismal thud against the wall, leaving a blotch of blood on the ice; only then did he drop him, saying:

"Let this be a lesson to you!"

The white man was never again going to insult anyone's wife. The white man was dead. Blood and brainy matter were seeping from his cracked skull, soiling the hides.

"Now see what you have done," Asiak said, still sniffling, while the crying children clung to her pants.

"Somebody didn't intend to kill him," Ernenek said, opening his arms disconsolately.

"But now his companions will be angry with us. They will probably drive us away."

Ernenek pondered for a while. "If we leave, they can't drive us away."

"Then let us leave at once. And since there is no telling what havoc the ghost of a white man is able to inflict, don't forget to eat a bit of his liver and to cut off a toe and a finger and put them into his mouth to conciliate his shade."

"Do you think I don't know how to behave?" Ernenek cried angrily. And while he started to fulfill the murderer's ceremonial in accordance with venerated custom Asiak hastened to cover every vessel that contained liquids or foods before the shade of the dead might contaminate them.

When the team was harnessed and the sled laden one of the white men came around to watch, and Ernenek grinned at him nervously; but the Eskimos took no notice of their departure. So they weighed anchor and rode back into their regions where they would be safe from the insults of white men.

Or so they thought.

The white men caught up with Ernenek in mid-summer. With the jawbone of a shark he had sawed a square into the sea that never thawed and, kneeling behind a windscreen of snow blocks, was peering with such intentness into the dark-green waters in wait for fish that he failed to notice the two men approaching with leveled guns till they voiced their presence.

"Ernenek, get to your big feet," the older man called. He was tall, with watery blue eyes in a sallow face. The younger one was stouter, with a hale complexion and glowing cheeks. Both had beards.

Ernenek jumped up. He was not visibly distressed by the guns and his big face broke into a grin that reduced his eyes to shimmering slits.

"Who ever heard of white men coming so far north?"

"We came all the way for you, just for you," the tall one said darkly. He spoke Eskimo, in a fashion.

"Really?" said Ernenek, his sanguine face beaming with joy. "I never saw you before, but I remember seeing this other one in the group of traveling white men a few moons ago."

"Right," the younger man assented solemnly.

"I'll guide you anywhere you want, but first I must fetch the traveling charms in my tent, which is inland, very close, and where you must be my guests. Then we can also take my sled which is with my wife, who is servicing the traps."

"You will come with us at once," the tall man said. "We have our own sled, that we left behind the island when we spotted you, lest you should suddenly disappear on seeing us come."

"Why should anyone wish to disappear?"

"You have murdered a white man, Ernenek, and mutilated his corpse horribly, and now you must answer for it," the younger one said in his ponderous fashion.

Ernenek laughed.

"I can answer you right now. Not only was I right, but he was wrong!"

"You will explain to those who are going to sentence you," the tall one said.

Ernenek frowned. "Are they his relatives?"

"No, but anyone who murders a white man gets a fair trial after which he is strung up to a tree with a rope round his neck till he dies."

Both spoke the language of the Men execrably and that must be why, Ernenek thought, they didn't get his point.

"I was right in killing him," he said patiently. "He insulted my wife abominably."

"Save your voice. We have a good team of dogs that will get us to the place of judgment sometime at the end of the coming winter. Then you may talk for a while before you hang."

"Somebody doesn't believe you want to kill him," Ernenek said, while his grin came back. "It would be silly taking a man on such a long trip during which he might give you trouble, instead of killing him right away, and you are not silly. Or are you?"

"These are our rules," the tall man said with finality.

He had heard that before, Ernenek had, that everyone was supposed to bow to the rules of the white men, who acknowledged no one else's rules. He didn't reflect whether that was right or wrong. He only wondered whether they could get away with it. With him.

So long as they were two, and had guns, they could.

The younger man took the snow knife which Ernenek had laboriously carved out of bone, the saw, the flint ax, the ice chisel and the spear, and dropped them into the fishing hole. Destroying implements that provided food and shelter and were so hard to make was a sin, and that was one thing Ernenek was sure about. He began straining his brain, but could think of nothing bigger than the two guns flanking him.

Fresh snow lay half a foot deep on the Glacial Ocean and progress was slow. Coastline, horizon, and the conical islands and icebergs emerging from the sea fields were partly erased by the summer haze rising in the watery sunlight. Not a wisp of vegetation was visible anywhere.

The white men's sled, heavily laden, all built of wood and with runners of gleaming metal that needed no icing, was anchored behind the island. The tall man was the driver. Ernenek, seated on a case between the two, critically considered the team in action—seventeen huskies, toughened by hard work on the trail and answering to Eskimo commands. They were not attached to the sled with an individual trace for each dog, allowing them to spread fanwise, but harnessed in single file. This was suited for driving through wooded country, but the failing of a single dog would affect the whole team. Of course the white men didn't know how to travel on the Glacial Ocean.

Nevertheless, at first they proceeded swiftly under the sun that never set. Once a family of seal basking on the ice looked astounded and guilelessly upon the passing procession, and before they could plunge into their holes for safety a couple of them lay hissing and flapping in their blood to the crack of gunfire.

Ernenek's mouth watered at the sight of all that fresh meat left by the wayside because the white men spurned what was best. And when they called a halt and pitched their cloth tent it was the food they gave him—beans out of cans, heated over the Primus stove—which depressed Ernenek more than anything else, for the only vegetables he relished were those he found in the stomach of the musk ox. He asked for some of the frozen fish, glazed with rime, that was fed to the huskies, and crunching that, with heads and bones, while the snow gritted between his teeth, he felt quite content.

Until the white men prepared their sleeping bags.

That's when they committed their gravest abuse: they shackled Ernenek like a dog. They put a chain around his hands and a rope around his feet and blissfully fell asleep.

When they awoke, Ernenek was furious. The fact that he was unshackled again didn't improve his mood. He didn't mind not having slept, for in summer he could go weeks without sleep; but the insult, the injustice of it all, was too much—and something had to be done about it.

While the younger man was strapping the cases and the older one, having shouldered his gun, was about to step onto the sled, Ernenek whirled round and crashed his fist on his head. There was a hollow sound, the man sagged, and Ernenek snatched the gun from him, brought it to bear on the other and pulled the trigger. But the gun failed to go off. Ernenek had fired but one shot in his life, and there were lots of guns about which he didn't know lots of things. By the time he decided to use the weapon as a club it was too late: the younger man had reached his own shotgun that stood against a case, aimed and fired it, and Ernenek felt a dull smarting in his arm. Then his fingers turned stiff with pain and the weapon slipped out of his hands.

By now the downed man had recovered from the blow. He kicked Ernenek in the ankle from behind, making him fall, then kicked his face till summer became winter. When day had returned to Ernenek, the younger man told him:

"Try that once more and you'll be shot through the throat."

He pulled down Ernenek's sleeve; blood flooded his arm and ran into his pants, but he didn't twitch under the flaring pain while the wound was being bandaged with strips of white cloth.

Before the journey was resumed he was shackled again and from then on his hands were freed only at mealtimes.

The sun made several turns, nine or ten or eleven, Ernenek lost count. In his arm the pain burned, stabbed, throbbed, radiating over shoulder and chest, and he barely touched the fish that was tossed to him. It had been warm so far, slightly below freezing, which increased his discomfort, and there had even been a snow flurry. Then the temperature dropped: the haze lifted, the puffs of respiration grew whiter, he could hear the click on the ground when he spat, his pain palled, and as he became more cheerful he reverted to his old habit of humming or mumbling to himself all the long day—and it was a long day.

A worsening gale churned up the ground snow and in the milky swirl the riders could scarcely see through to the head dog of the long-strung team. Then and there, Ernenek thought, he would stop and build a shelter. But these men always chose the hard way to nowhere. He noticed the driver was shaping course for the coast, probably wanting to seek shelter under a bluff or a hole in the cliff, and he began feeling alarmed, for they were heading straight for a promontory where, owing to the strong undercurrents, there was the danger of meeting cracks with open water during a storm.

"Have you at least all your charms with you?" Ernenek asked the man at his back, who shook his head in denial. Ernenek became panic-stricken. Traveling without charms, that ultimate of all follies!

The driver turned around and, patting his gun, said, "These are our charms."

"To travel safely on the ocean you need at least an ermine's tail and a seal's eye. If you take somebody's shackles off, he will build you an igloo."

But they were deaf to reason and Ernenek began uttering magic phrases in a hurry and touching his genitals in order to avert disaster.

But it was too late.

The team leader swayed and swerved with such abruptness that the second and third in the line went ahead before also swerving, entangling their lashings, and the others stumbled over them pell-mell. Into the jumble of legs and bellies swept the heavy sled, and nosed clean into a chasm brimming with water.

Ernenek, eyes wide open with alarm, was the first to jump off, and the younger man behind him followed his example. But the driver on the box went down with the sled.

Six huskies had broken out of their harnesses and stood on the brim, barking inanely into the lapping water. In the gap, some ten feet wide and as long as the eye could reach, dogs and harnesses were floating round the blue, gasping face of the tall man who flapped his arms helplessly.

"Help me get him out," his companion cried.

Ernenek smiled at this new foolishness. "He is a dead man. Besides, the sea would get angry at us if we took him out."

A blow with the butt of the gun reminded him that white men don't listen, but tell; so he went down on his stomach and stretched out his arms over the gap while the white man pinned his legs. The man in the water got a hold on Ernenek's shackles, but the drenched clothes had prodigiously increased his weight and he was pulled out with difficulty.

He was put on his feet but never spoke. As he stood in the ripping wind the soaked clothes instantly stiffened, the water on his furs froze into myriads of tiny icicles and his face became gloved in a crust of frost through which the eyes glittered glassy and enlarged. His companion began hacking away at the frozen clothes with his hunting knife, cracking them open and cutting them off, but the body also was encased in ice. From the injured knees blood rushed forth, thawing up the ice crust from within and dyeing it a brilliant red.

Then the blood also froze.

Ernenek shook his head. Had they even to die the hard way? But at least this man had died on his feet. When he dropped on the ice his body gave a glassy sound.

His companion stood in a daze.

Ernenek grinned triumphantly. "Our position is not good," he announced full of glee, and added, "When you come to a strange land you should take your wives but not your laws with you."

Without a word the white man rolled his companion back into the water. Then he took stock.

"We have six dogs and a hunting knife," he said with sudden grimness, shouting against the wind. "We'll eat the dogs and continue on foot."

Ernenek answered with a big laugh, for the white man talked as if he still were in command. And he laughed because he was free.

Far as the eye could reach, and way beyond, there was nothing but ice-paved ocean, ice-capped islands, and barren, deeply frozen land.

CHAPTER SIX

The Road to the North

"SOMEBODY is going his own way," Ernenek said. "You may go yours or come along, as you wish. But my tent is much nearer than your post."

The gale was tossing them about and the white powder clung to eyebrows and nostrils, forming small icicles that hurt when removed.

"My hands are clumps of ice," the white man said. "The mittens must have touched the water."

"It was stupid letting that happen. Just as stupid as throwing your friend back into the sea without taking his knife and his clothes."

"Why?"

"We could have eaten his clothes, at least what was made of animal wool and skin. And if you people had clothes like the Men, which are waterproof and sewn with sinew that swells when soaked, making the seams watertight, your friend would be alive. From now on you had better watch your step, for your next mistake is likely to be your last. And remember: one rip in your clothes or your boots means the end, since we have no sewing kit."

"What is to be done?"

"First take these shackles off. Then somebody will show you how to make friends with frost and let it help you rather than hurt you."

After his shackles had been removed Ernenek flung them into the sea. Then he pulled the white man's mittens off and turned them inside out, baring a thin crust of ice.

"Give me your knife, and hold your hands inside your trousers where it is warmest." He scraped the mittens with meticulous care and dried them with snow, making sure with his upper lip that they were free of frost.

"My hands have no feeling at all," the white man said, all cockiness drained from him. "They are dead!"

"Not yet. Not quite."

Ernenek called the huskies. They refused to approach. When he tried to catch them they escaped. He sat down and talked to them, full of play, munching some snow. The moment one of them ventured within range he grabbed it by the nape of the neck and cut open its belly, while its mates howled and moaned.

Obeying Ernenek's orders the white man plunged his hands into the dog's steaming belly and kept them there.

"My fingers hurt terribly," he said after a while. "As if countless needles were piercing them." He was ashamed because, despite his efforts at controlling himself, he felt his eyes fill with tears. It was the sharpest pain he had ever experienced.

"It is the announcement of life returning to your hands," Ernenek said. "And, with life, pain comes back. Only death is painless."

Meanwhile, under the skin of the dog's belly he had found a little fat with which he greased his own and the white man's face. Then he extracted the fuming liver, bit into it voluptuously and passed it to his companion.

"Eat it before it freezes," he said, grinning, his mouth purple with the liver, and the white man bit into it staunchly.

Ernenek pulled out the bowels next. Surely, he too had tasted better ones, like those of the reindeer always crammed with lichen, but it was foolish of the white man refusing anything at a time like this.

"We'll need the meat for the building of a sled," Ernenek said, feeding the guts to the team.

He skinned the dog, running the knife between flesh and hide and tearing at the pelt. Racing against the frost which was invading the tissues he boned the carcass and cut the meat into thick strips, carefully separating the sinews and putting them inside his pants to keep them warm and wieldy. Then, sitting on the pelt, he began to carve the breastbone with the knife.

Time passed. The sun, a pallid ball of fire, kept circling above the horizon. The white man trotted around for warmth. Ernenek worked, humming to himself. The steel knife made carving easier than the sharp splinter of flint-stone he was wont to work with, but he realized he had to handle it with care lest it should break, for he had already chipped it.

Out of the bone of the dog he fashioned a crude barbed spearhead. Then he wet the dogskin in the water, spread it on the ice and rolled it tightly, pressing it while it froze, inserting the spearhead into one end and tying it with the sinews of the dog. The wet skin froze quickly. He welded

75

shaft and head with another quick dip in the water, and had a new spear made of dogskin and bone.

"On our way down, not far from here, it came to pass that somebody heard the bellowing of seal," he said, flinging the dog meat on his shoulder and striding forth over the sea. "The gale has erased the sled tracks but the dogs will lead us."

Although the dogs had been afraid of the men before, now they were afraid of being left by themselves and went along, and soon, following their own scent, they were preceding the men.

The seal Ernenek had heard were a short way for him but a far cry for his companion. They were in open territory from where they might survey the approach of bear. When the dogs stopped and began to bark and burrow Ernenek dropped his load, drove them back, downwind, and gave them the order to be quiet. They whimpered and whined a little before they fell silent, cowering.

With his hand Ernenek carefully removed the surface snow till he had bared a hole somewhat larger than a hand.

"This is a blowhole."

"So small? How can the seal come up across the thick ice?"

"The hole widens below, till it gets wider than you are tall. Now somebody will wait for a seal to surface while you walk around in a circle. That will drive the seal toward the center and away from other holes."

The white man obediently stalked off and Ernenek waited motionless, spear poised, eyes fixed on the opening. He watched it shrink, the ice rim closing in on the center. On the last water patch a shivering film appeared, then the opaque skin of frost.

Abruptly, Ernenek felt weary and cold, which frightened him. He had never felt that way. But he had eaten too little for too long. He, who could devour a whole seal calf in one sitting, had fared on nothing but some miserly dog food during many a turn of the sun, after having been abused and manhandled and wounded. And all that because some people carried no charms, couldn't mind their own business, and were clumsy in doing it!

His thoughts were at the lowest ebb when there was a splintering sound and a hiss, and a small geyser of water and air and ice chips spewed into his face. For an instant a gleaming, black, bald head popped out and a pair of huge eyes glared at him flabbergasted. The surprise was mutual. Already the head was gone, gone so quickly that Ernenek might have thought it a dream had it not been for the water wavering in the freshly opened hole.

Ernenek froze into immobility. He almost stopped breathing, straining to pierce the dark waters, since he didn't have his floater to tell him when the seal approached the surface. The seal had no necessity to come up this way again, for it kept open several holes from which to draw air. A seal is wise. But it is also curious. A seal, too, is only human, and Ernenek was sure that curiosity would win out in the end.

He was sure, pretty sure, that those two blotches he saw looming beneath the water surface were the seal's big eyes and not an excrescence of his own excited imagination. He sent off a quick prayer to that effect toward his own personal guardian spirit, to which every Man reverts when he is suspended between life and death, and struck.

The spear caught, and caught the seal where Ernenek had aimed it, and where it was best: into the upper lip.

It was a heavy, mustachioed male and Ernenek shouted for support, holding the spear fast with both hands while the quarry struggled. The white man came trotting stiffly to his aid, helped kill the seal and widen the hole with the knife, and together they pulled up the catch.

First of all Ernenek tore an eye out of the seal's head and buried it within his jacket.

"Now we are safe!" he exulted. "This eye will protect us from further mishaps." And henceforth nothing could dampen his high spirits.

"Why do you melt snow in your mouth and spit it into the seal's mouth?" asked the white man who had retained the perpetual curiosity of his race despite cold and discomfort. Ernenek shook his head in the face of such abysmal ignorance. Even a child knew why. "The soul of this animal will now tell the others that it has received a drink of sweet water, so they will come up and try to get caught by us, hoping to get a drink too. Seal are always very thirsty, as they live in salt water."

He sucked the black, oily blood from the fuming wound, flensed the kill, fed the dogs a few scraps of skin, and cut out the stomach from which he retrieved living seafood that even the white man relished, seasoned with the sour stomach juices. He relished a little less the liver and the heart, and bluntly refused the thick, fat guts, despite the assurance of Ernenek, who ate several yards of them, that they were a treat tasting like mussels.

"Now go ashore and get some turf," Ernenek said. "Remove the snow with your boots, then use a stone to scrape the turf from the frozen ground. It won't be easy."

"Why do you need turf?"

"Do as you are told without arguing. Arguing uses up a lot of strength."

"If I see the reason it is easier to comply. I am very tired."

"Somebody is making a sled. But the snow on the ground will stick to the runners unless they are shoed with ice. Ice won't stay on the runners; turf will. So the runners are first coated with turf, then the turf can be iced and the runners will glide without friction. Now you see the reason."

While the white man went stiffly on his errand Ernenek cut the meat and blubber into strips, as he had done with the dog, all the while knifing at the ravenous huskies that gave no peace. Then he cut the sealskin in two, lengthwise, dipped the halves into the blowhole, rolled and pressed them while they froze, and so obtained the runners for his sled.

But he needed another seal for the traces of the team and after a wait that might seem long to those measuring time by hours instead of seasons he bagged another, smaller one, whose skin he cut into ribbons that he knotted together while they were still warm and wieldy. He laid the strips of meat across the runners in the guise of crossbars, lashed them with the sealskin ribbons and welded the joints by squeezing water over them by means of the dog's tail.

Whalebone made keener runners. Driftwood made lighter crossbars. But not much.

By that time the white man was back with two pocketfuls of powdery turf. Ernenek mixed it with hot urine and plastered the paste thickly over the bottom of the runners, shaping it smooth with his mitten. Then, being out of urine, he melted snow in his mouth, squirted it on the dog's tail and glazed the runners with an even coating of ice. He worked all the while with great concentration and knitted brow. The layer of mud must be thick, but very smooth. The water must not be too warm lest it thaw the mud; not too cold lest it freeze before spreading. The coat of ice must not be too thick or it wouldn't stick; not too thin or it would crack.

When he was satisfied with his work he harnessed the dogs in his own fashion, throwing the traces artlessly about their chests and attaching each of them individually to the sled—the center dog on the longest trace, the outer dogs on the shortest ones. But he didn't step aboard without returning the bones of the seal into the water, mindful of an agreement the Men had entered into with sealdom since time out of mind, whereby the killers had to return to the sea the skeletons of the killed—otherwise the seal would never again allow themselves to be caught.

He stuck the speartip into the nearest dog, that gave a howl, electrifying its teammates into action and making them realize that they had better start pulling with every pound of their strength, and a few ounces to boot, if they half cared for their bones; and the sled began to glide on the ocean.

Northbound.

They rode on for a long time. At first they felt strong and warm with the meat and blubber of the second seal, and the gale glided off their freshly greased faces. But with hunger setting in, the cold began biting through to their bones, forcing them often to jump off the sled and trot for warmth. When the dogs began to stumble Ernenek called a halt.

"We must let them rest. We can't afford to lose any."

"I want to take a nap," said the white man.

"Not without shelter. You wouldn't wake up. It isn't far now."

"I'll never reach your tent. My weariness is as big as the ocean."

"Somebody will spear other seal, and if you would only cram yourself with blood and blubber and liver you would feel strong and warm. Food replaces sleep."

But the sun had made two complete turns and they had stopped several times to rest the team before the dogs smelled out another field of blowholes. While Ernenek lay in wait, the white man drove the sled around him in a circle. But no seal surfaced. They could be heard hissing and coughing in every hole but where Ernenek lurked.

"There!" he cried, alarmed, giving up at long last. "Word must already have spread that people have killed seal without returning their bones to the sea, as you did from the sled, and now the others refuse to be caught!"

But the white man had not heard the charge. He had dozed off and the unwatched huskies were gnawing savagely at the crossbars.

Ernenek jumped with anger and swore at the folly that allowed dogs to retain the sharpness of their teeth. He shocked the white man into wakefulness, then bore down on the team and smashed their fangs with the handle of the knife, while his companion kept their jaws unlocked with the spear shaft.

They drove on without food and sleep in the endless day, in the great winds that scoured the roof of the earth. Ernenek ate up his seal-eye talisman and fishing amulets, assuming it could make no difference whether he wore them on his body or inside; after that he chewed on a bit of sealskin and made the white man do likewise, for he knew from experience that there was nothing so vivifying as the skin of sea animals. Meanwhile, he cursed Asiak for her thoroughness, for if she weren't such a meticulous dressmaker he might now find bits of dried meat and fat clinging to the inside of his garments, but they were gleaming smooth within by dint of tanning, scraping and chewing.

He needed the coastline for landmarks by which to set his course and never let it out of sight. Sometimes a blizzard forced them to call a halt and improvise an igloo with nothing but the small steel knife, or to hole up in a cliff.

The white man followed doggedly. He had thinned down and the lines of strain and stress lay deep in his haggard face. His whiskers were full of ice, his ears swollen, his lips chapped, his limbs stiff. But he was still strong enough to refuse to die.

He used to believe he had nothing more to learn about the white land, not only because he knew that temperatures as low as minus ninety-eight degrees Fahrenheit had been registered in this region, that the altitude of the sun was twenty-seven degrees at noon and eleven degrees at midnight, that a four-head family like Ernenek's had to themselves, statistically, sixteen hundred square miles of territory, and more such facts and figures, but also because he had learned to distinguish between the sweet ice of precipitations and rivers, brilliant and always full of air bubbles, and the frozen ocean crust which was an ugly, opaque gray. But his practical notions didn't extend much farther. So he didn't know that old coarse-grained snow contained more water and tasted sweeter than fresh snow, nor that sea water lost its salt content and became drinkable after being frozen over a period of time.

Much less would he have recognized dead seal in the snowy hummocks by which Ernenek halted, saying:

"These are the seal you shot on your way down." He bared with the knife a scarred brown hide. "We should have an ax."

He gave great kicks to the carcass but couldn't loosen nor pry it from the ice on which it was frozen. He succeeded only in cutting off the tip of a flipper, which he defrosted in his mouth after pulling out its nails. It contained a lot of fat, his mouth watered, and in his greed for more he broke the knife and cut his hand. While the huskies licked his blood from the ground and cast covetous glances at his soaked mitten he pulled a tuft of hair from his jacket and laid it on the gash to staunch the blood. Then he redonned his mitten and joined the huskies on the ice, clawing and gnawing at the carcass.

It was like sucking on a stone and he soon gave it up, but had a hard time persuading the crazed dogs to resume their stations, and they snarled and snapped when he tried to work some sense into them.

They were in a bad state. One was limping, another had an eye closed from a blow, the third was festering at the mouth, the fourth yammered incessantly, and all had blistered or cut their unprotected feet, as they had long since used up their shoes, and the salt of the sea ice ate into their sores. After a further spell the fifth, that had seemed the least affected so far, stretched itself out on its flank and refused to budge, impervious to Ernenek's encouragements.

Sitting on their haunches and drooling from their mouths the other four glared with yellow eyes as Ernenek reasoned with their stricken mate with the aid of the spear. A little blood appeared where the spear had pricked it. As at a signal its teammates pounced. There was no stopping them, nor did Ernenek try. Patiently the dying husky glared into the darkening day.

When they were feeding more slowly Ernenek cut out the tongue with the stump of the knife. The dogs' bellies were swelling while they tore and gulped without chewing, wolfing the meat and hide and cracking the bones with their blunt teeth till not a scrap, not even the harness, was left. Then they curled up and slept. Ernenek let them.

For a little.

The sun made several turns before they abandoned the Glacial Ocean and climbed ashore. Here the grade and the broken ground prevented sledging with so reduced and worn a team, and Ernenek smashed up the sled against a rock, salvaging the meat and letting the dogs have the runners.

The stiffly frozen crossbars could not be chewed, only sucked on slowly, and he wanted to kill one of the dogs; but as they were on their guard again, approaching them proved impossible, and he cursed his foolishness for having freed them too soon of their traces.

Abruptly, however, his face gladdened and he beamed on his companion. "Somebody just remembered that not far from here he made a meat cache years ago!"

"But the meat will be frozen stiff like that of the seal and we won't be able to get at it," the white man said surlily.

"Somebody always cuts up meat before burying it and

lays stones under it to prevent it freezing fast to the ground." He went ahead and the white man trudged after him, grim and taciturn.

A stream of invectives announced that Ernenek had found what he was looking for—and that it was gone. A family of wolverines had been there first, had dug the ground causing the heavy stones to topple downhill one by one, and had feasted on the find, leaving nothing but a handful of gnawed bones and the spoors of their paws.

When Ernenek was tired of saying unflattering things about wolverines and wanted to resume his march he got wind of a fox. He looked for its spoors till he found them, and trailed them in the hope they might guide him to the guileless cubs in the lair. Instead he was led to a cache of auklets that the fox had made in the bird cliffs for the winter, and the purple, well-decayed meat was a comfort to his stomach and filled him with new strength and good humor. But the white man couldn't be persuaded to touch it. Moreover, his nailed boots afforded a poor hold on the slopes. He slipped once too often and refused to get up.

"You give up too easily," Ernenek chided him. "One night a man somebody knows, lost in a blizzard, ate his own feet, which were useless anyway because they were frozen, to get the strength to return home. We still laugh each time he tells the story."

Ernenek shouldered the white man, but soon had to put him down again: the strain was beginning to tell on him.

"Somebody will go ahead and lead the dogs along with a piece of sled meat, so they won't attack you. Suck on this crossbar meantime and don't fall asleep till somebody comes back with food and fresh dogs."

And he trudged off humming.

He found his tent of hides where he had left it, at the foot of a huge boulder, and his home team of huskies welcomed him noisily and then sniffed suspiciously at the four shabby, scrawny beggars that had followed him.

First little Papik toddled out of the tent, broader than he was tall in his fur garments and white boots, bouncing and squealing for joy. Then came Asiak. She had spread in body and in spirit in the past few years, but her burnt almond eyes still smiled pleasantly in the fat of her face. Over her shoulder Ivaloo, safely strapped on her mother's back, looked out in blunt astonishment at the big hulking figure that called itself her father.

"You were away many sleeps," Asiak said casually. "You must have caught a lot of huge fish. A woman will prepare the sled so we might haul in your catch."

"Somebody has made a miserable catch," Ernenek avowed for the first time in his life.

The white man was not asleep when they went to fetch him. Nor did he fall asleep on the bed of moss and hides in the tent. Nor after Asiak had served him bowls of tundra tea and meat charred over the lamp. He had done without sleep for a longer time than he had considered possible, and some cog, some thread within him had become defective, and for all the weariness of his body there was a flaring wakefulness in his brain and sleep eluded him completely.

Not so Ernenek, whose body and memory hastened to dismiss the past hardships. He lost no time in glutting himself with whatever meat was at hand, adding tallow to aid digestion, and when he felt too heavy to stand up he stretched out on his back and let Asiak feed him some more. When he was unable to swallow he droned off into sleep.

It didn't disturb him in the least when, tugging with hands and teeth, Asiak pulled off his boots, and her scraping his feet clean with a knife barely altered the key of his snoring.

From his bed of hides the white man watched Asiak do her home chores, while Ivaloo, almost constantly strapped to her back, slept placidly or craned her fat little neck at him. Little Papik often stood curiously by the strange guest, touching his hairy face and laughing the warm and frequent and rootless laughter of his people.

After sleeping a good turn of the sun Ernenek awoke, bent on refilling his stomach and spoiling for the hunt.

"You are not like the natives we trade with," the white man said pensively.

"It is as you say. Once we tried to sleep in the trading post and nearly choked. It was so hot the ice in the bucket almost melted."

"Certainly," said Asiak reminiscently, "life is more agreeable and amusing in the hot South. In summer you can paddle in a kayak, and there are big crowds of people, and such a variety of foods. The women lead lives of luxury and ease, wearing light suits of fox fur, fine socks of spotted seal and soft reindeer boots that reach barely to the knee instead of our heavy bear suits and boots of rough seal."

"And men with harpoons float on the ocean in big umiaks and chase white whale and narwhal!" cried Ernenek, kindling at the thought.

"And the air is full of bitter little mosquitoes while the sweet-tasting lice crawl all over you, and man and wife can have a lot of fun picking them off each other and eating them."

"But hunting the big bear and spearing the great seal of the North is more exciting," Ernenek said, "even if it is too cold for lice here. And now it is dangerous for us to go where the white men trade."

"Would you like to?"

"Certainly, especially now that it is forbidden."

"You have saved my life, Ernenek," the white man said, "and I wish to straighten things out so that you need no longer fear my companions. But you will have to stand before a judge. I will help you explain things."

"You are very kind," said Ernenek, happy.

"You said the fellow you killed provoked you?"

"So it was."

"He insulted Asiak?"

"Terribly."

"Presumably he was killed as you tried to defend her from his advances?"

Ernenek and Asiak looked at each other and burst out laughing.

"It wasn't so at all," Asiak said at last.

"Here's how it was," said Ernenek. "He kept snubbing all our offers although he was our guest. He scorned even the oldest meat we had."

"You see, Ernenek, many of us white men are not fond of old meat."

"But the worms were fresh!" said Asiak.

"It happens, Asiak, that we are used to foods of a quite different kind."

"So we noticed," Ernenek went on, "and that's why, hoping to offer him at last a thing he might relish, somebody proposed him Asiak to laugh with."

"Let a woman explain," Asiak broke in. "A woman washed her hair to make it smooth, rubbed tallow into it, greased her face with blubber and scraped herself clean with the knife, to be polite."

"Yes," cried Ernenek, rising. "She had purposely groomed herself! And what did the white man do? He turned his back to her! That was too much! Should a man let his wife be so insulted? So somebody grabbed the scoundrel by his miserable little shoulders and beat him a few times against the wall—not in order to kill him, just wanting to crack his head a little. It was unfortunate it cracked a lot."

"Ernenek has done the same to other men," Asiak put in

helpfully, "but it was always the wall that went to pieces first."

The white man winced. "Our judges would show no understanding for such an explanation. Offering your wife to other men!"

"Why not? The men like it and Asiak says it's good for her. It makes her eyes sparkle and her cheeks glow."

"Don't you people borrow other men's wives?" Asiak inquired.

"Never mind that! It isn't fitting, that's all."

"Refusing isn't fitting for a man!" Ernenek said indignantly. "Anybody would much rather lend out his wife than something else. Lend out your sled and you'll get it back cracked, lend out your saw and some teeth will be missing, lend out your dogs and they'll come home crawling, tired—but no matter how often you lend out your wife she'll always stay like new."

Summer had slipped away. The sun had widened its course, hiding below the horizon and giving a hint of night for a longer spell at each turn, till it was gone; and the long night came, bringing with it an immense weariness of all living beings, so great that even the ever-hungry ones like Ernenek lost interest in food.

So the small family folded their tent, packed guest and bundles onto the sled and built their winter igloo over the water.

When Ernenek and Asiak dozed off to the rumble of the ocean the unattended lamp went out, and there in the great darkness the great sleep came to the white man at last. It came to him gradually, in thickening shifts, like fog, like night. Sometimes in the twilight of consciousness he sensed Asiak strike fire and light the lamp, sew and scrape, remove the clump blocking the entrance and feed the huskies that grew fat in the tunnel, or Ernenek putter with his hunting gear. When he was offered blubber or fish he swallowed it obediently, having found that it gave more warmth than a stoveful of charcoal, and even when he was presented with a stone bowl brimming with black seal blood veined with oil he downed it politely.

At winter's end when day broke and Ernenek began whetting his blades and Asiak crawled ever again out into the open to watch the sunlight hoisting itself slowly up to the roof of the world, the white man was well enough to travel.

"We'll drive you back," Ernenek said. "It will be as easy as becoming a father."

And they left in the gloom of dawn.

It was late evening when the white man sighted the wood cabin that was his destination and asked Ernenek to stop a little way off.

"You don't want to be seen here by anyone, Ernenek," he said, alighting.

"Why not?"

"Because they are looking for you. Because there might always be some trader who knows you and might tell them your name."

"By now they must have forgotten about somebody."

"White men don't forget. They'll all keep looking for you till they find you, and there's more of them than caribou."

"Maybe those who knew somebody have died. White men die easily."

"They write your name down in big books. The men die and the books remain."

"However," Ernenek said patiently, "we want to see a trading post again with its funny goings-on, after traveling all this way. Once we decided to have nothing to do with white men, but since knowing you we have changed our mind."

The white man's face assumed a pained look. "You go back to your region, Ernenek, and I will tell them I saw you dead. This is the only way they might, not forgive, but forget you."

Ernenek shook his head grinning. "They will understand when they hear a man's explanations, just as you did."

"Even if some of them should understand they couldn't help punishing you, Ernenek, because their rules are stronger than they. Their rules have grown greater than those who made them. Do you understand?"

"No."

"Then I'll explain in a different fashion." He took a deep breath. "Listen: I don't want you with me because I am tired of your company and of Asiak's laughter. I will put a bullet through your big stomach the moment we reach the post, and feed Asiak and the little misfits, that surely are your children, to the bear, because I hate bear so."

And while Ernenek's jowl began to drop in surprise, the white man kicked him in his lower belly and crashed his knuckles into his grieving face. Then he turned around and made a tilt for the cabin—pigeon-toed, because he wore high Eskimo boots that Asiak had made him during the winter.

Ernenek looked after him utterly baffled, scratching himself where he had been most hurt. After all he had done for him! After letting him have the best part of his hunt, and a good part of his wife!

He turned to Asiak, who was also too flabbergasted to speak, and they wondered mutely, once more, about the oddness of white men.

Then he resumed his place on the sled, and turned the dogs around, and headed for the horizon.

PART II

CHAPTER SEVEN

•

The Long Journey

SHORTLY after they had separated from the white man Asiak found herself once more with child.

Since the couple already had their hands more than full with two children to raise they doubted whether it would be wise letting the new one live. So they decided to keep it should it be a boy, but if a girl they would return it to the ice.

Asiak bore a girl.

But when they saw she had hair like the sun and eyes like the midsummer sky and skin like new snow, they fell in love with her. No doubt, it was their winter guest, the white man, who had fathered her, and Ernenek was mighty proud that his wife had borne him a white man's child.

They named her Hidjoodjook.

Although all Eskimos doted on their children, spoiling them to the utmost, and punishments and beatings were practically unknown, yet it is doubtful if even an Eskimo child ever experienced such pampering as that little bundle of sky and sunshine and snow.

But one ugly, stormy day, while still too little to know what she was doing, Hidjoodjook toddled off alone into the weather. Asiak, who was dozing a lot because it was winter and because she was pregnant again, didn't notice her absence till the storm had erased her tracks. Ernenek was out fishing. So she hunted on her own for the little explorer, stumbling and shouting in a blizzard so fierce that her house dog failed to pick up the scent.

The same dog led Ernenek to Asiak many hours later.

He found her bleeding under a snowdrift. She had miscarried and was delirious. Of Hidjoodjook no trace was ever found, as if Sila, the bad man in the sky, had lifted her from the face of the earth. So she couldn't even be buried, like other children, together with the head of a dog, and there was no one to escort her little soul to the distant land toward which all Eskimos are traveling.

Asiak never got quite well again. She became pregnant every year and each time she miscarried. This drained her of her strength, and youth, and laughter. Her knotty hands began to ache in the joints and she was no longer able to carve those fine sewing needles of bone that had been her pride. Her teeth, worn down to the gums by the chewing of hides, were indeed suited for preparing the thin aukskins that sharp, young teeth would damage, but unable to soften bear- or sealskins.

She was slowly growing into a useless, burdensome woman, and aware of it.

She began to long for southern warmth and comfort, but since the white men were after Ernenek she prevailed upon him to confine their existence to the silent North and give a wide berth to any place where they might encounter white men or such Eskimos as traded with white men.

So the luxury of driftwood was superseded entirely by bone and horn and walrus ivory; their bows were made of antlers instead of whale, their snow goggles of walrus tusk instead of wood. And they met only Polar Eskimos like themselves, and few of them, for their number was as small as their territory was large, and every blue moon a nomad family of Netchiliks.

Yet these contacts were sufficient for them to know that the world was changing.

The number of white men's trading posts was increasing; they mushroomed here, there, everywhere, and at each meeting with other Eskimos the talk inevitably reverted to the white man, and his ways, and his wares. The white man was spreading in the white land, sending ahead his fame, carrying with him his firearms, his firewater, his foods, his languages, his goods and gods, his lares and lores; bearing gifts unasked and taking things unasking, making rules and breaking rules, and leaving in his wake a mad whirlpool—sometimes joy and riches; sometimes desolation, imprisonment and death.

Long stretched the arm of his regulations, and he was a smart Eskimo who learned quickly to abide by them. White men had hung a native merely for killing a scoundrel who had stolen his wife, as any man would have done, for a wife may be traded, rented or borrowed, but not stolen. And it was known that in some of those regions where white men had settled, no native was permitted to kill more than three seal a year, though his existence was based on seal oil and seal blubber and seal meat and sealskin, while the white hunters wiped out whole nations of seal, just for the sake of their skins and the oil in their livers, abandoning the meat to the gulls and neglecting, of course, to return the skeletons to the sea. (Small wonder seal was getting scarce!)

No, there was neither rhyme nor reason to what white men did.

And besides his rules and his wares he had also introduced his multifarious diseases. Venereal infections, influenza, tuberculosis, and above all measles wrought havoc among organisms uninured to germs, and men, used to besting the Polar bear and to enduring long treks and blinding blizzards, succumbed easily to the invisible enemy in the blood; and in some settlements, where a larger number of white men accounted for a wider spreading of diseases, epidemics were known to have destroyed eight Eskimos out of each ten in a few weeks.

Yet, though all about the white man was not good or understood, everything about him fascinated the Eskimos —with the attraction of the depths. And even when remote from him in time or distance they could not drive him from their thoughts, and sometimes those that had not quite surrendered to the lure of the new modes and manners were bothered in their minds more than those who had. Even the Angmagssaliks, even the Netilingmiuts, even the Itas, even the Atkas, even the Unalaskas, even the Palugvirmiuts, even the Nookalits, even the Wootelits, even the Igloolingmiuts, even the Copper Eskimos, even the Caribou Eskimos, even the Netchiliks, had succumbed and lay low, helpless, under his spell; they could no longer do without his knives, his guns, his Primus stoves, his firewater, his sweets, his ribbons, his mirrors, his beads—that required constant replacing or refilling, and had to be paid for with hides, and fish oil, and labor.

Only the sparse group of Polar Eskimos went on living in the way of their ancestors, still too artless to lie and too true to be good. Yet the white cancer had begun plaguing their hearts also, and Asiak sensed often that the silences of her loved ones were clamorous with yearnings and their barren nights peopled with the forbidden wonders.

When at the age of seven Papik slew his first seal—just a cub that had not yet learned to swim—Ernenek made him lie flat on his stomach and then dragged the kill over his back, so that the animal might not be afraid of him and warn the other seal to beware of Papik. But it took several more years before he was a full-fledged hunter, able to provide for a family.

And the family was soon going to need him.

Ernenek met with an accident from which he never entirely recovered. He slipped during a bear chase and tumbled down a slope, breaking a lot of ice and also his back. He lay helpless for many moons and when he finally was able to get up he could neither bend nor stoop nor sit: his spine was stiffer than frost. He had to lie flat or stand upright, and it was always comical seeing him twist round on the couch and push himself up along the wall when he wanted to get to his feet, and it afforded him and his family a lot of food for laughter. He could walk and run, but not for long, and lifting weights drove pains into his back and loins that sent him groaning onto the couch.

At times his pains were so bad that he was barely able to laugh them off.

In his forties he was an old man, indeed the eater but no longer the hunter he used to be, bearing the marks of his long journey through time. Deep were the scorings on his face, sunken and leathery the cheeks, abundant the snow on his mustache that hung in sparse threads over his puckered chin. And there was wonderment in his eye when he beheld Papik—the arrow he had discharged through Asiak's bow—for he was so much as he himself had been in his youth.

According to his mother's guess Papik was sixteen or seventeen when he began greatly to resemble his father, big and muscular as he had grown. And he was as boastful as his father, but not quite; as reckless, but not quite; as bluff and blatant, but not quite.

Never could be, being also Asiak's son.

Ivaloo was shorter than her brother, not yet fully grown but already sturdy and broad-chested. Her lips were, like Asiak's, large and full without being turgid, but the slant of her vivacious eyes was Ernenek's. She was curious but unwitting, eager but ignorant, untouched by civilization, education, regimentation, communication, transportation, aviation; untilled soil, unplucked flower. The virgin wax of her mind was susceptible to people, for she had met so few, and her mood was wayward as the wind. But laughter always won out.

Until she met a young man named Milak.

It was during a summer hunt inland that she made his acquaintance. They exchanged only a few words, and none of them friendly.

"Somebody doesn't need a man," Ivaloo said.

"If you don't need a man you are not a woman," said Milak.

"What is somebody then?"

"A child, with the brain of an auk and the heart of a wolverine. Only a child can expect to do without a man."

"A child likes your conceit because it keeps her warm with merriment," said Ivaloo, and her laughter broke fresh.

What louts these Northerners, reflected Milak, being a Southerner. Only Asiak bore traces of gentility: she must be of Southern stock. But Ivaloo and Papik were crude as their father. Almost. No one could be quite as crude as Ernenek. Barely one sleep earlier, when Milak had told him after a hunt, "Mine is a miserable catch compared to yours," Ernenek had had the cheek to answer, "Indeed!"— for what little show of modesty he had laboriously acquired in the past had got lost in the years when he had been out of human contacts.

Was it surprising if such a man's daughter, instead of calling herself the most worthless female that ever laid eyes on such a powerful hunter, now laughed at him? But that's the way she was. Milak could take it or leave it.

And he took it.

"You see," he tried to reason, his wan young face working for control, "your father isn't much of a hunter since he cracked his back, and your brother will soon find a wife of his own to provide for."

"A girl is able to hunt and fish as well as any man," Ivaloo said.

"But who will do the sewing? You can't do everything. And as a woman you are not permitted to kill a seal, nor can you run after bear and bend over fish holes when you are swollen with child or carry one in your hood. Once you have a child or two you will have to look for a husband."

"Why?"

"Because your brother can't provide for so many people!"

"Maybe you can't, but Papik can! We are Northerners, and the only thing at which you foreign weaklings beat us is your conceit!"

Milak flushed under his layer of soot and blubber. He got up and stamped about and spat, while she regarded him with interest. He intrigued her. He came from the land of the short shadows, the hot, gay, fascinating South, where the sun and the musk ox and the reindeer come from.

"So a man will go back alone," he said finally, sulking, and retreated in good order toward the sun.

Ivaloo dreamed of men powerfully built, blustering and gay, like her father, and Milak was nowhere near it. He was a successful hunter, being quick and deft, but not muscular enough for her fancy, almost frail looking compared to Eskimos in general and Polar ones in particular. He seldom laughed, and his nervous, changing face betrayed the constant battle of thoughts.

Yes, the more she mused over it after he had left, the more she disliked him. And her dislike was constantly on her mind, in her dreams as well as in her waking hours. Until one day she said to her mother:

"It seems in the South there are angakoks capable of influencing the weather and the hunting season, and of curing people. We might even see some of those white men who have mysterious powers; maybe they can repair Father's back."

"Father is better off with a stiff back than healthy among white men."

"Then we won't go where the white man occurs, only far enough to meet a good angakok."

Asiak watched her, worried and fondly. "Maybe you are right," she said with a sigh. "Somebody is tired of having a husband who lies on his back when he comes back from the hunt and moans over his pains like a woman in childbed. Milak said that in his village is a powerful angakok. Let us look him up and see if he can chase the evil spirits from Father's back."

Ivaloo flew to embrace her and snuffed at her, sleeves flapping, and Ernenek and Papik joined in her joy and immediately started packing.

But Asiak's face remained dark and stormy.

As they traveled to the southward in the dusk of dawn it was Papik who sat high in front wielding the long whip against the wind while Ernenek was in the back, standing upright on the last crossbar.

The earth was still asleep, the dwarf vegetation had not dug itself out yet from beneath the wintry crust, and what animal life breathed underneath didn't show a hair or, if it did, being ice colored, couldn't be spotted in the gloom of dawn; except the bear, that were too proud to hide.

In this waiting world under the fading stars the quick metallic panting of the team punctuating the silence was drowned out at times by the lowing of the gale scouring the great plains, swaying the huskies and bending the riders with its power; except Ernenek, of course, who couldn't bend an inch.

When the weather forced them to drop anchor and erect a shelter it was Papik and Ivaloo who did all the work and Ernenek all the criticizing.

"Never mind," Asiak would say. "He always knew everything better." And the children laughed into the blizzard, heaving the blocks in place and filling the chinks with snow, while Ernenek stamped about, snorting and sneering. Within the igloo they lay close together, lined side by side like salmon set out to dry, and the soft puppies were allowed to nestle between their masters unless they started licking the grease from their faces.

"When a man's back is repaired he will show you how to build an igloo," Ernenek would say, tossing on the narrow couch.

"Yes, you know how to build them small outside and large inside," was Asiak's answer. "The angakok may be able to repair your back but not your old age. You are soon ripe to be set out on the ice."

They all laughed at this, except Ernenek whose huge sense of humor had a way of vanishing mysteriously whenever he was the butt of a joke.

"Asiak used to speak quite differently when I returned from the hunt," he said resentfully. "How times have changed!"

"Times haven't, but you have."

This was good for more laughter, till drowsiness and digestion came to drown their gaiety.

But there were times when all were restless with anticipation, as if they knew that the journey would work a change not only in scenery but in their lives. And times when the sleepless children asked their mother the eternal questions—and there was nothing their mother couldn't answer.

"Where does all the snow come from?"

"Snow, my little one, is the blood of the dead."

"And thunder? Somebody always wonders what causes thunder."

"The spirits rubbing their hides against each other when they have an argument. Usually female spirits."

"And lightning?"

"When the arguing spirits knock a lamp over. That's why lightning and thunder come together."

"And shooting stars?"

"Star dung, of course. What else could they be, little one?"

"Of course. But somehow it never occurred to me. And who made the first people?"

"The Black Raven."

"And who made *him*?"

"The ice crust cracked open and out of the sound the Raven sprang into being. He was black, because it was night. He soon felt lonesome sitting all alone in the world, and so he made little men out of balls of sod. The men then, getting mighty bored because they had no one to scold, made women out of little balls of snow."

"And where is the Black Raven now?"

"He is dead. The little men grew up and slew him."

"Why?"

"In order to eat him—before having had time to find out that he alone might have prevented them from dying."

"That reminds me of something I long wanted to ask: where do the souls go when the people die?"

"They have three paradises to go to: one in the air, another in the earth, the third under water."

"What does a soul look like?"

"Like the person who wears it, only much smaller."

"How small?"

"The size of a little auk."

"And what do people's names look like?"

"Like souls, but smaller still."

"Have you ever seen souls and names?"

"Not yet, but my mother has."

"Did she really?"

"Why would she say she did if she didn't?"

"And where do the names go after people die?"

"They float miserably in the air till they find new bodies

to house in. That is why you must always give new-born babes or dogs the names of the dead."

"But where do all the new babes and pups come from?"

"Usually from the Moon Spirit, who looks like a man and has the power to make all females barren or fruitful. He sees also all the breaches of taboos and punishes you for them."

"Is he as wicked as they say?"

"He is even worse, and extremely whimsical. There is only one worse than he: Sila, the man in the sky who makes the sun go down and sometimes carries off a human being."

"Why are the spirits so bad?"

"They are like people: some are good, some bad. How could there be good ones if there were no bad ones? Sedna, for instance, the woman with the tail of a seal who commands all the creatures of the sea, is very kindhearted: she sends us all the good fish. And there is the Air Spirit, who is neither good nor bad, and effects the weather changes. Is there anything else you wish to know, little ones?"

"Is there anything *else* to know?"

Asiak reflected a while before answering. "You are right. What else is there to know?"

While they traveled sunward, the sun spiraled up to meet them halfway. They watched the liver-colored horizon begin to bleed, grow purple, crimson, red, red tinged with gold, red tinged with yellow, red tinged with day— and then the triumph of the sun dripping with gore, reddening the ice, splashing the sea fields and hills and isles with its lifeblood, till it was bled white, hanging wan and anemic over a monotonous earth.

Fog rose. Snow fell. It was high noon—summer.

All day they rode over the solid sea, traversing great plains beneath which the water rumbled, filing between conic islands and icebergs jutting from the ocean, following strips of land indented with glaciers and many-cleft mountains rising bluffly from the sea. They saw the first tiny mosquitoes, the number of birds increased steadily as they approached their largest breeding and mating grounds, the shadows grew shorter with each turn of the sun, and the winds bore the distant fragrance of the open sea, the smell of mist, of earth, of herbs and flowers.

The glare of the sun was fierce, the ice shivered under the runners and one could hear the rumble and rush of the sea close underfoot. They met ever more rifts in the sea that forced them to swerve from their chosen course, and when they saw the forbidding stretch of pack ice ahead they had to abandon the ocean and continue their journey overland.

Here progress was wayward and arduous, leading across yawning gulfs and below frowning heights. The sled rumbled and bumped on the uneven ground and they had to hold on to uprights and straps. Projecting bits of ice always became entangled in the traces. When they descended a glacier the anchor had to be cast and the dogs attached behind the sled to act as brakes. Uphill, everybody had to push at the uprights.

"The angakok will have not one but two backs to mend," Asiak said after each such effort, and her children would double up with laughter.

They watched the sun, which had never succeeded in hoisting itself even near the center of the sky, tire of its endeavors and begin to sag, growing larger and richer as it neared the horizon, growing into a glorious gold that turned saffron, pink, rose, red, purple, mauve, finally to plunge below the line in a trail of blood. Day was done. Fall was on. Light subsided while colors were gone, and the earth shivered before the menace of night.

And in the quietness of the world waiting for darkness, in the sunless light of evening, the travelers were just in time to behold the spectacle of the liquefied ocean flecked with slowly drifting icebergs and floes, new and almost incredible to Papik and Ivaloo.

"It looks just like the sky," cried Papik.

"Yes," said breathless Ivaloo. "Like the sky with water in it."

CHAPTER EIGHT

End of a Man

THE village, laid in a cove and cowering under a spit of land, was bounded by great snow slopes and glaciers which gradually lowered into the sea, and beyond rose ranges of ice-covered mountains with black and brown foothills. Papik and Ivaloo had never seen such a numerous community: there were three square-shaped communal houses, semipermanent dwellings built of snow and sod and the bones of whales, and a handful of spear-shaped, one-family stone dwellings.

And there even was a house built entirely of wood.

The curiosity was mutual. Most villagers had never set eyes on inhabitants of the mysterious North. So they clustered round the crude outlandish sled entirely made of meat and bones, and warily at first, then with increasing familiarity, opened the bundles and rummaged in them. They found several bear hams that they appropriated with shouts of joy. Ernenek was delighted, but not for long.

To his great chagrin an event was taking place that dwarfed that of his arrival. During the summer, plowing its way through the broken ice, a huge smoking-boat had steamed into the cove, disembarking six white men and unloading heaps of cases, coal and wood. The boat had left immediately, for fear the sea should close in and entrap it till the next summer. (What of it? Why were the white men in such an unhealthy hurry?) The cases contained mysterious utensils and instruments. There also was enough wood to build a house made of boards from the floor to the roof, and in it the white men had spent the past weeks, warmed by a coal-fed stove and living on tinned foods and bottled drinks.

Asiak was relieved to hear they weren't enforcers of white man's rules, but explorers, interested in the lay of the land and not the names of the Men.

They were waiting for the ocean to freeze in order to push onward, upward, across and beyond the land of the Polar Eskimos. They planned to journey in native fashion, as a self-sufficient unit—traveling light, with few provisions, building shelters from the ground, extracting fuel and food from the ocean as they went.

All this Ernenek learned from Siorakidsok, the local angakok, in whose snowhouse the entire community had gathered to hear what news the North wind brought.

Papik and Ivaloo were shy of the new faces and unfamiliar surroundings, and dizzy with the crowd of people. Yet for all her dizziness Ivaloo saw Milak very clearly, though he sat as far away from her as the room allowed. He also was looking at her—with hungry eyes and a frown that came and went.

Siorakidsok was a skinny, spry little man whose eyes blazed in deep-sunken orbits beneath a bulging forehead. He liked to say he was twenty generations old, which just meant very old, for among the Men not even a master mathematician was able to count so far. He was paralyzed from the waist down and hard of hearing. It was only owing to his great reputation as an angakok in intimate alliance with the good and evil spirits that he hadn't been set out on the ice. He had no teeth and his granddaughters —or perhaps they were great-granddaughters—Torngek and Neghe, prepared his nourishment with their own teeth and fed him mouth to mouth.

Torngek, the eldest, had two husbands; being second-rate hunters they had decided to share the duties and joys of married life. But Neghe's husband was a great hunter, the family's real provider and the community's unnamed leader. His name was Argo and he gloried in having so many dependents, for everyone looked upon him with envy and admiration.

He not only had a shotgun that would have functioned if he had had ammunition for it, but his household boasted the only Primus stove that worked whenever kerosene was available. They had used it only for brewing tea quickly, but since the arrival of the white men they had also cooked their meat a few times, just to find out what the white men saw in it. Boiled meat they could endure; but if charred over a fire they could neither stomach it nor even stand its smell. For these villagers were Southern only to the Polar Eskimos, to whom everybody was a Southerner. To the white men's knowledge the settlement was the northernmost outpost of human existence, and its inhabitants had never before seen, and barely heard of, white men.

Except Milak, a restless wanderer, and Siorakidsok, who had seen everything including the Man in the Moon.

Right now a huge kettle filled with snow and chunks of Ernenek's bear hams had been set on the Primus to boil, for the white men had yielded some of their kerosene and promised to come.

In a corner stood a large stone trough into which everyone passed their water, valuable for tanning and washing. Some men and women smoked soapstone pipes and the fumes of their tobacco from dried niviarsiak and bilberry leaves mingling with the smells of cooking and kerosene were offensive to the Northern nostrils.

But while Asiak wrinkled her nose and her children stared in mute bewilderment at the foreign ways, Ernenek was radiant with the joy of change and new companionship.

"Why are the white men going North?" he shouted for the third time into Siorakidsok's large but insensitive ear, standing under the lofty ceiling of snow supported by beams of whalebone.

"They want to see what there is," Siorakidsok answered at length, grinning with his black toothless mouth.

"A man can tell them what there is up North! There is ice, large plains of ice, and land also, all covered with hard snow and ice. Above the ice is wind. On the ice, and sometimes in it, is bear. Beneath the ice is fish and seal." Ernenek spoke between snatches of laughter. "Tell them not to waste their time. There's nothing else."

"They want to see with their own eyes. They don't believe what the Men tell them."

"Why?"

"Maybe they don't understand the Men's language well enough. They say they want to make drawings and images of what they see. They say," and here Siorakidsok bent forward with a face-splitting grin and his withered skin broke into a netting of wrinkles, "they want to measure the cold and weigh the winds."

Everybody was convulsed with laughter, even those that had heard it before.

"They have promised a gun and two steel knives and a lot of ammunition to every Man who goes with them, and so everybody is going, even the boys and the old," Siorakidsok went on. "But it was not easy convincing the white men to take women along. They thought they could travel without women."

This also caused widespread hilarity.

"How can anyone be so stupid?" continued Siorakidsok who, thanks to his deafness, suffered no interruptions, so that his speeches were frequent and long. "Who lights the lamp while the men bury the sled? Who prepares the tea while they hunt?"

"So what was decided?" Ernenek asked impatiently.

"Who dries their clothes while they eat, and repairs and softens them while they sleep?" Siorakidsok went on undisturbed. "So somebody suggested that at least those women that are not pregnant should be taken along, and at long last the white men were agreed."

"Pardon a female for talking," Asiak said, "but somebody thinks your suggestion denotes great wisdom."

This remark fell on Siorakidsok's good ear and he nodded in full agreement with her. Here was a wise and a discerning woman indeed!

"Somebody will go on the trip with the white men," Ernenek said.

Asiak reared her head, quick, but didn't say a word. It was Ivaloo who, overcoming her shyness, spoke up:

"The white men can't use one who has a stiff back. You made this journey to have it repaired, not to start on a new one."

Ernenek stamped his foot. "A stupid girl, that hasn't even yet laughed with men, talking this way to her father! The world is really going to the dogs!" He turned to Siorakidsok. "You know how to heal. Will you heal a man's back, so that he might leave with the white men?"

Siorakidsok's deafness reached an all-time high. Ernenek had to step closer and Argo also went over to him and they repeated several times, shouting into both his ears, what was expected of him.

At great length Siorakidsok nodded understanding.

"The white men," he said, "have an angakok in their midst who can do remarkable things. He sticks fine needles into your arm so that all feeling leaves, and cuts deep into your flesh without shedding blood. Try the white angakok, and only if he fails will somebody disturb the spirits of the Men."

"Let us see if the white men are ready to honor us by partaking of our foods," said Argo. "It is for them we have put the bear meat to cook. They have never tasted bear."

When the six white men entered they spread silence round them. Papik and Ivaloo were terrified and awed. At the time a white man had wintered with them they had been too small to remember him now, but they had heard that white men had caribou feet; these wore boots, so you couldn't tell, but you could tell they had inordinately large hands. They were all rather young and rugged looking, with thick beards. A couple of them spoke good Eskimo for white men. They explained that the expedition could use Ernenek, provided his back was well.

The medical visit was brief. Ernenek let his pants down and the white angakok, one of the youngest in the lot, making elbowroom about himself against the tight circle of onlookers, knocked and pressed and prodded Ernenek's powerful back, tickling him and making him giggle. Then he straightened up and sentenced:

"There is nothing to be done."

Everyone looked expectantly at Siorakidsok: it was his turn.

"An angakok must first consult with the Moon Spirit. Unlike a white man, an angakok is very stupid, and wishes to take advice," he said.

But since a consultation with the Moon Spirit would have taken several turns of the sun, and neither Ernenek nor Siorakidsok nor anyone else wished any longer to delay the banquet, Siorakidsok was easily persuaded to forego his consultation for once and trust his own experience.

"Somebody," he announced, "will let blood out of this man's back, and with the blood the evil spirit that has entered his body will flow out. Torngek, fetch my instruments!" And while his favorite granddaughter rushed to comply, Siorakidsok began to pound Ernenek's bare back with his fists.

When he thought the back felt ripe he took from Torngek a lancet of flint, thrust it into the fifth vertebra and smote it with a heavy rock, then pulled it out. A gush of blood followed. The surgeon bent forward, put his lips to the wound and sucked with all his might.

"Now bring me a lamp," he said, licking his lips. He took a piece of flaming moss from the lamp, slammed it on the wound and fanned it with his breath. When the moss had burned itself out he called:

"Cover your heads and open the roof so the spirit can fly away!"

The stopper was pulled from the smoke hole and everybody covered their heads with their jackets, because spirits hate to be seen fleeing, and Ernenek's back was pounded anew to a chorus of yells and shouts designed to hasten the spirit's departure.

When the voices were getting hoarse, Siorakidsok gave permission to uncover, and Ernenek pulled up his pants with a sigh of relief.

"Can you bend?"

"No," Ernenek said sheepishly.

"That means there are more demons left within you," Siorakidsok said reproachfully, wiping the sweat from his brow, "because an angakok distinctly saw one spirit fly away. We'll have to do it soon again, but next time not without first consulting the Moon Spirit."

Thereupon everybody returned happily to their places, the men in an inner circle, the women in the background, ready to echo their husbands' merriment.

All were very hungry by now and the long-awaited delicacies were passed around—musk-ox stomachs full of moss and lichen, unplucked eider ducklings that had been rotting in seal guts crammed with blubber, their flesh enticingly purple from the chemistry of decay, fermented caribou brain, raw intestines of birds, slime scraped from the aukskin and smothered with the human urine used in tanning, maggoty larvae of the caribou fly, and the white men's keks made more interesting with tallow and deer droppings.

The kettle on the Primus stove was beginning to boil and loud laughter and voices filled the room with an air of social amenity.

"Any man would consider himself fortunate to be left alone with so many women," Siorakidsok tried to console Ernenek who looked blacker than winter.

"But it will do him no good if his back is stiff," said Argo, drawing gales of laughter.

"Can he be dangerous to women, or can't he?" one of Torngek's husbands inquired of Asiak; but she evaded the answer with laughter.

"It is said that a man who can't be dangerous to a bear can't be dangerous to a woman," Argo said. "Or is it the other way round?"

Under other circumstances Ernenek would have been delighted to be in such brilliant and witty company. But this time he was irked. It had never happened before that he wasn't considered fit to participate in a great venture, and the Southern delicacies took indeed the wrinkles out of his stomach but not the bitterness from his heart.

Standing with legs outspread and arms akimbo in the murky daylight that filtered through plates of clear ice and windows made of seal and caribou bladders, he cut an impressive figure in his shaggy bear clothes. He was not the tallest but easily the broadest of the lot. His jowl was fearful to behold, even now that a few teeth were missing, the muscles above his ears reached high on his skull, and when he spoke, a powerful diaphragm went to support his conviction.

He snorted, spat half across the room and burst out loud enough for even Siorakidsok to hear him the first time:

"It is shameful that a pack of Southern weaklings who need countless dogs to hunt bear, and prefer seal because it is safer game, should talk so to one who has killed more bear than there are auks in the sky, and with nothing but his spear and his wits. Has any one of you ever wrestled a bear after the spear broke, and slit his belly open with a knife? Or pulled a walrus out of the water by its nose and mashed its brains in with his bare fist?"

The peals of laughter that greeted each sentence sent the blood shooting to his face. He didn't realize that the laughter was only due to such blatant self-praise, an unheard-of boorishness.

Asiak was aware that Ernenek's deportment in society left much to be desired. She was gravely embarrassed and kept raising her eyebrows at him in quick succession, trying to attract his attention, but he did not choose to comprehend the signals. His children, instead, were angry with the crowd. To them it seemed that at any mundane event Ernenek's presence should be considered an ornament and honor. Papik jumped to his feet, shouting, "It is as Father says," and Ivaloo added furiously, "That you don't know what sort of man he is only shows your boundless Southern ignorance!"

And Ernenek, so they might start knowing what sort of a man he was, lifted the big teakettle and smashed it demonstratively on the floor.

The rough blanket of snow was old and threadbare and Ernenek's footfalls made crunching sounds as he trudged up into the hills, heading for the glacier valley. He was tired from the trip, weak and dizzy from the bloodletting, and his back hurt, shooting rays of pain into his legs. But a pain is easier to carry than an itch, and he itched to show those despicable Southerners what a real man was capable of.

That was the reason he had left the gay company at Siorakidsok's house.

The village sounds reached clearly through the crisp air. When it was warm and about to snow they didn't carry

111

far; but in cold air a man's voice might be heard a whole day's journey away. There was the uproar of a dog fight and a woman's litany and the harsh grating of a jawbone saw and the joyful shouting of children tobogganing down a slope on a sealskin.

And right before his nose the persistent humming of myriad tiny mosquitoes that he sucked in as he went and crushed between tongue and palate to savor their bitter-sweetness.

When he reached the nether rim of the glacier he started keeping his eyes fixed on the ground till he discovered bear spoors, and tracked them up the glacier bed. They must belong to a very hungry bear, for they were close together, with the toes pointing inward, denoting a thin animal. But he lost them on rocky ground. Then, spotting bear droppings in the distance, he was led to fresh spoors.

They took him through a small gap between rocky boulders. The steep foothills and the ground that had been exposed to the rays of the sun during the summer were dry, but the shady spots carried stale snow and ice. The ache in his back increased with the strain of the ascent, spreading to his loins, and he leaned heavily on his spear. To be unencumbered he had left his bow behind, but in his boot he carried his sharpest knife.

On a patch of snow behind a boulder a bear cub was toying with its own hind leg. Its pelt was short and woolly and its tiny eyes looked with interest into a world whose dangers it had not explored. Ernenek dropped to the ground and began to whine in soft prolonged tones. The cub looked up and studied the strange form in the snow. After a while it approached, sniffing the air, its shiny little nose moving about like a finger.

The unexperienced odor of man meant nothing to it.

But the first meeting with him was abrupt and painful. Ernenek's hand shot out and grabbed the cub by the soft, warm throat; then, groaning with pain, he got to his feet by pushing himself up along the stone wall. The cub squealed hoarsely, showing its blue tongue and clean teeth and wriggling madly in Ernenek's clutch. When it grew tired of squealing, Ernenek pricked its tight belly with his spear and the cub squealed again delightfully.

At last the mother came.

Ernenek heard her pant on top of the boulder under which he stood, and backed up, waiting for the onslaught. She scuttled down with a dull rumble in her throat and made a tilt at him. Ernenek flung the cub against her nose, gaining time to grip his spear.

As she rose on her hindquarters he struck into her mouth.

She clutched the spear with both paws in an effort to pull it out, but broke it instead, for the spear was so designed to leave the barbed tip in the quarry, and only a piece of the shaft remained in Ernenek's hands. Barely a gasp came from her, a flow of blood gushing and steaming in the cold air, a gurgling sound, and down on her side she went, while the cub scampered off yammering. Ernenek glanced about to see whether the male was coming.

He was.

But he hadn't spotted the enemy yet nor his dying mate; he had merely heard the cub's distress. His vision ran poor third to his sense of smell and hearing, and he was warily sniffing the air.

In his youth, Ernenek used to wet his upper lip with his tongue to sense the direction of the wind; but sensitiveness had left him, so he plucked a snarl of hair from his pants and tossed it up into the air. He was safe: the bear was almost exactly upwind.

Regaining the spearhead embedded in the throat of the female that had rolled away from him to die was no laughing matter for one who couldn't bend and didn't wish to be heard. He was screened from the male only by the rock wall. So he stood still and waited. Being downwind, he could hear the beast breathe above him, sometimes holding its breath in order to listen. It was moving away. Soon he would be able to retrieve his spear stump, then invite the bear to a dance. He had a good chuckle to himself, thinking of the villagers' faces when they saw his prize. Yes, he was still able to give a bellyache to a whole village!

The number of mosquitoes had increased, attracted by the odor of blood. He inhaled deeply, sucking in a swarm of them. Before he knew it one had blundered into his tonsils, causing him to cough.

From there on things happened swiftly. Having betrayed his presence, Ernenek flung caution to the wind and rushed to his kill, dropping to the ground and beginning desperately to extricate his weapon. But while the worms of fear cut capers in his guts and he shot anguished glances at the rock above him, some recondite corner of his brain enjoyed the show madly, thinking of the good story it would make back at the house.

And already the male hove into sight, waltzing down the sloping slab of slate, slower, warier, with more purpose than the female. He was unusually long and thin and his nails scrunched and grated on the rock.

Ernenek had barely regained his spear and was pushing himself up along the wall when the beast, covering the last stretch of ground in a quickening jog trot, rushed him, rising on its hindquarters and opening its forepaws. Ernenek aimed vaguely, more by instinct than design for which there was no time, at the hissing cavity towering above him. The gory spearhead entered the bear's mouth and came out through the cheek. It failed to deflect the attack by an inch or delay it by a heartbeat. This was the moment for Ernenek to drop on his back, roll off and reach for his knife.

He fell on his back all right—and stayed there.

Eight hundred pounds of growling vengefulness crashed on him, squashing him against the ground, pinning him fast. He rammed his left forearm just in time between the gaping jaws while the steamy breath was already scalding his face. He felt his thigh crushing the inaccessible knife.

The beast was gnawing through his sleeve, mangling his arm, but he kept it hard across the jaws. He had learned to extract pleasure from physical pain in order to endure it. With a movement of the wrist he got rid of his right mitten and searched the animal's underbelly for its small genitals.

He put a grip on them and pulled.

No bullet through the heart could have more instantaneous effect. The beast relented its bite with a gasp and staggered to its hind legs, clutching at its groin. Blood rushed forth through its forepaws. Then it toppled to one side, doubled up, and began to spin on the ground, reddening the snow all around.

Ernenek struggled to his feet. His arm hurt badly now that the lust of battle was gone, and his crushed loins tugged him groundward, but exerting all his will he succeeded in hoisting himself up. Beads of sweat on his brow proclaimed the effort and the pain.

But if he was to die he would die on his feet.

From the severed artery of his arm the blood spouted in ten-foot jets to the rhythm of the pumping heart. He could observe the ebbing of its power. With what strength remained it was all he could do to press his left elbow against the pain and watch life run out.

Mosquitoes danced before his nose. A ptarmigan cackled. From the village came a woman's call. A weasel was spying an invisible quarry. A swarm of sweet-singing auks were feeling their wings against the breathless sky before leaving for the South.

Could this be death? So clear? So simple? And so without warning?

CHAPTER NINE

End of a Woman

PAPIK and Ivaloo wept and whined and beat their heads against the wall, but Asiak, neglecting manners, advertised no grief. She only took her children into her arms as when they were little—and little they were in her arms, as she snuffed at them and bathed her face in their tears.

The body had been found by Papik, who had followed his father's tracks and carried him back into Siorakidsok's house in the hope that the angakok or the white men might bring him back to life. Papik knew nothing about death, or he would have left the corpse where he found it, saving everyone a lot of bother.

Only girls that had not yet reached puberty and old women past the age of fertility were permitted to touch the corpse, wearing mittens. They washed it in urine, lashed it in a doubled-up posture, tied its hands and feet in order to hamstring the ghost, and plugged the nostrils with moss.

"Why can't we simply take the body back to the hills as we always do with our dead?" Asiak asked Siorakidsok who was acting as master of ceremonies. "The animals will dispose of it and nobody will be bothered."

"Since some foolish person has thought well of contaminating this house with the corpse we must now do everything in our power to protect ourselves from the ghost that might be floating in the room," Siorakidsok said worriedly.

Over the naked corpse, tied doubled up, a hole was pierced in the roof as a passageway for the soul. All the women wailed frightfully, in between praising the dead unstintingly in order to ingratiate his shade, while the men belabored the dogs with heavy sticks so that they, too, might contribute to the general grief.

The white men also came to see the dead, but they didn't cry nor even beat the dogs.

Among them was a preacher who had joined the expedition in order to carry the Torch into those Northern reaches not yet illuminated by the Christian Faith. Silence fell when he stepped into the house. He was a rugged-bodied man of medium height, with a florid complexion and a blond mane which had earned him the name of Kohartok, or Colorless Hair. His soft-flowing beard was reddish and his eyes a pure water-blue.

He neared the dead man and made a speech. He must have spent considerable time learning Eskimo, for he seemed to have little difficulty in expressing his thoughts.

"Another sinner is going to his last resting place," he said, looking at the circle of listeners. "But will he find rest? I doubt it, for this man is going without having made peace with his Maker. When a thing is too late it is too late. So may this death serve as a warning to those who have not yet surrendered to the Eternal Father. Let it be a call to one and all to repent of their sins, for the Kingdom of Heaven is at hand. I have been telling you this ever since my arrival, for this is the purpose of my coming: to spread the Seed among you. I heard this man was a great hunter. But what good will the many bear he has killed do him now? He certainly won't require their hides in the eternal fire in which he is roasting. Wouldn't it be preferable if he had spent less time chasing bear and more time bent in prayer, asking God's forgiveness for his sins? The Kingdom of Heaven, rather than the Flames of Hell, would now be his, and he could be buried in the Christian cemetery alongside Alinaluk with a cross over him, instead of being hidden in pagan earth. Now we can only pray that God may have mercy on the poor sinner's soul. Amen."

"What did he say?" Ivaloo asked Asiak. "You know what the white men mean by their words."

"Hush now," Asiak whispered. "Somebody hasn't the slightest idea what he meant, except that he called him a great hunter. Each tribe has its own habits and those of the white men are very strange. It must be their way of placating the ghost."

For five days all the women helped to mourn for Ernenek, grieving loudly, beating their breasts and tearing their hair. Neither Asiak nor her children were permitted to rest or sit down during that period, and nobody, not even the dogs, took nourishment, except on the sly.

On the sixth day the corpse was sewn into skins and the burial took place.

Argo stepped through the wall, breaking a hole in the snow house through which the funeral party filed out. The breach was repaired at once in order to prevent Ernenek's shade from retracing its way into the house, causing mischief as dead souls will.

The bulging coffin of skins was put on Ernenek's sled, led by Papik who clubbed the dogs lustily, while the women kept crying, moaning and gesticulating. Behind Asiak and Ivaloo came Siorakidsok, two of his sons-in-law carrying the rug on which he sat.

Out of sight of the village the procession stopped and the men began digging a grave. The summer had thawed the soil down to one foot on which vegetation had sprouted, but underneath it the ground was frozen and could not be dented; so a rectangular enclosure of stones was made, into which the coffin was laid.

Papik strangled Ernenek's favorite dog and rested it at its master's side, together with Ernenek's hunting gear and a lamp with a lot of wick and blubber with which to brighten the great dark and warm the frozen earth. Then all the diggers cast their mittens into the grave and erected a steep cairn over it with heavy rocks for protection against prowling wolves and enterprising wolverines.

Then Siorakidsok held his graveside oration:

"Now that you have covered the dead man with stones you must cancel his name from your talk and his image from your minds forever."

The air was gusty and the listeners only caught snatches of his elegy, according to the way the wind fell.

"You had five days in which to weep all the tears worth weeping for any man and to extol all the deeds any man is able to accomplish. From now on there shall be no more of that. This man should be envied for the life he led, not pitied for his finish. All lives come to an end, and whether they end a little sooner or a little later, what matters, since they end? Whatever ends is short. And is it bad that life is short? No, for it is the knowledge of its shortness that makes it valuable. And this man made the most of his."

Ivaloo buried her face in her mother's hood. Sobs and moans could be heard by even the hardest ear. Siorakidsok beamed. This was a brilliant, successful funeral indeed.

"He saw his children grow up. He hunted the big bear. He ate considerable amounts of food, and usually the best. It seems he even killed a white man! May your children grow up to be as strong and as lucky. Now remember to sweep out your tracks carefully on the way back: we don't want to be trailed by his spirit. This man is bound to have a particularly baleful spirit." Everyone nodded and mumbled in agreement.

"As soon as you have returned to your mansions, be sure to wash from head to toe, in case the shade of the dead has sullied you. Don't forget to sprinkle water on the ground so the dead may have a drink, and when you eat, don't forget to drop morsels of meat on the floor so the dead may eat, too. Then build enough sham snares around the village to give his ghost the fright of its life should it ever try to come back!"

Hereupon the gathering dissolved, Siorakidsok making sure personally that the rear guard erased all tracks.

"Why did you put soot on your and your daughter's eyebrows?" he asked Asiak when he came back to the house and found her sitting in a corner with Ernenek's pants on her head and busy with her sewing kit.

"We are not allowed to stitch for a long time because using pointed instruments may injure the ghost. But the men who left their mittens in the grave need new ones urgently, as they are about to leave, and blackening one's eyebrows is a good protection against the ghost's revenge. So I was told by my mother, who had it from her mother."

"Women, women," Siorakidsok scoffed. "Always stupid and superstitious! You are quite right putting your husband's pants on your head to appease him, but the only effective safeguard against the sewing taboo consists in drawing with your needle a circle on the floor and to remain inside it till you have finished your work."

"It is wonderful how wise you are!" And Asiak hastened to comply.

The strip of gray ice that had fringed the coast for several days had meantime turned white, meaning it was thick enough to carry the weight of men and sleds, and the spirit of frost moved along the face of the waters, conquering more and more ocean surface with each passing hour.

Papik also was leaving with the expedition.

"Somebody will get himself a gun and steel knives and learn the white man's ways, little one," he told his weeping mother when his sled was ready. "Then he can get all the meat and skins you want."

"Somebody wishes you wouldn't leave, little one. But if you do, don't worry about a silly old mother, but think of Ivaloo and see that she makes a good wife to a good man when you come back."

Here Milak, who was standing behind Papik, burst in.

"No need to wait till then. Somebody needs a woman to look after his garments on a little journey he is about to undertake, and it is possible that he will take Ivaloo with him."

"It is possible, but not probable," Asiak said.

"Why?"

"Ivaloo is the worthless daughter of a worthless mother, and hasn't learned yet how to scrape skins well, nor how to sew with small stitches. She is too little and inept to be worthy of a real man."

"But somebody would let you have a valueless lamp if you let her go, a few colored ribbons of no account received from the white men, and some paltry meat."

"A certain old woman already has a lamp, is not worthy of wearing colored ribbons, and is not very hungry. No, no, Milak: keep your treasures, and an old woman will keep her daughter."

Meanwhile, Milak was carving Ivaloo up with his eyes. "But if somebody comes back from a trip, as he might, may he then take Ivaloo with him, or at least laugh a little with her?"

"It is not impossible."

"When somebody comes back," Papik told his mother, "it is possible that he will take a woman of his own. Somebody saw a suitable girl, but she ran away every time he tried to speak to her."

"It's a good sign. Her name?"

"Vivi."

The white men were champing at the bit. But so often did the Eskimos have to unload the sleds and remake their bundles, remembering what they had forgotten, so often did they return to their homes for a last cup of tea or a last laugh with those women they left behind, so many traces and straps and harnesses were found in need of repair at the eleventh hour or broke at the instant of departure, that before the expedition was finally underway, the world had darkened considerably.

Forgetting conventions, Asiak and Ivaloo escorted the expedition for a stretch, together with a few children too young to know manners. Glacial winds were scouring the coastline under a sullen sky.

Thirty-five Eskimos with as many sleds, ten women and five white men were on their way on the ice strip, the teams racing one another. Papik was in the lead. His dogs were lean and strong from the recent journey while the village huskies were fat and slow as yet.

"Why didn't you let a daughter go with Milak?" Ivaloo asked, trying to keep up with Asiak.

"Because it is not wise traveling with white men. They are dangerous and crazy. A woman couldn't stop Papik but she still can stop you."

"Now somebody will never get a husband!" Ivaloo cried sulkily. "Milak was the only young man who ever wanted a girl."

"Milak was the only young man who ever saw you. Don't worry, little one: you are pretty, men like pretty women, and as soon as you have grown a little stronger, able to carry a good load on your back, you will easily find two and even three husbands who will be glad to take you on."

"Are you sure of that?"

"Very sure. You must remember that a small girl is worth so little that more often than not she is killed; but for the same reason she's worth a lot as soon as she grows big, because there are few of them. Only when a woman gets to be my age she's worth nothing."

After Asiak and Ivaloo had lost sight of Papik in the murky gloom they returned to Siorakidsok's house, where they found Neghe and Torngek preparing tea before retiring.

Neghe's husband, Argo, would suffer no dearth of

women: all the men who had their wives with them would be proud to lend them to him, and so Neghe wasn't worried about his well-being. But Torngek, her fat old sister, was in tears because her two husbands were always treated like stepsons, and she wanted to accompany them. But Siorakidsok was too fond of her comfortable disposition to let her go.

"A useless old woman and her ignorant daughter are soon going to build an igloo of their own," Asiak announced.

"Nobody can blame you for wanting to desert a crippled old man and his ridiculous granddaughters," Siorakidsok said after he had caught the drift of her speech. "However, it will be unusually quiet with no men in the house and only a bunch of silly women and children left in the village. And last summer it came to pass that a lot of musk ox blundered against the arrows of Argo, one's worthless grandson-in-law, the sealing also was good, a big whale was beached, and food stores are plentiful. Would you do us the honor of partaking of some of our paltry provisions and of brightening the house of an old man with your presence?"

Asiak was swept off her feet and replied in style.

"It is indeed a great honor you are showing us, but isn't it a shame to waste such fine food and quarters on two foolish women? No, no, they should build their own igloo!"

"An old man feels flattered that you accept his meager hospitality."

They drank tea, wrapped themselves in skins and dropped off to sleep.

But Asiak soon woke up.

"Ivaloo, little one," she whispered, gently shaking her daughter. "A mother knows you need guidance for another while and that you shouldn't be left alone. But nobody will have pleasure in taking care of a mother who is old and useless."

"What do you want to say?" Ivaloo asked, looking up through curtains of drowsiness.

"For a woman who all her life had the privilege of bestowing gifts upon others it isn't dignified to accept hospitality from strangers."

Ivaloo was still dazed with sleep. "What do you intend to do, Mother?"

"To leave, little one. But don't ever think a mother loves you less only because she went away. You are well off here, sheltered and fed."

Ivaloo was slowly awakening. "Where do you want to go, little one?" she cried, alarmed, thrusting her arms around her mother. "You are not also going to leave me?"

"Hush, Ivaloo. You'll wake the others. Go back to sleep. You look very tired. A woman will join her husband in the distant land where all the Men go, and there she will wait for you."

Ivaloo wanted to say more but weariness tugged at her lids and she allowed her mother to wrap her up and tuck her in. Asiak snuffed a little at her face, then quietly slipped out of the house.

The weather had changed for the better and the sky was a pure and pallid evening color. A woman hailed her as she went toward the sea. She smiled absently, nodding a greeting. The remnants of walrus and narwhal and of a white whale lay on the beach beside two large umiaks and a fleet of kayaks, all carefully covered with skins, and long lines of salmon were drying on racks.

She stepped forth onto the frozen strip of ocean and walked toward the water.

She got interested in two small boys deftly paddling their fragile kayaks of sealskin and driftwood on the rivulets of water between the ice floes, sometimes shooting arrows at the auks and guillemots that, flying in tight formation or

stringing out in endless line, skimmed the water in search
of fish.

The boys were buttoned up in waterproof gut jackets
which, tightly fastened about their waists and faces and
secured round the hatch, made them part of their kayaks,
allowing them to capsize their craft and then right it again
without taking water aboard. Showing off before Asiak
they turned swift somersaults in the water, upsetting the
kayaks bottomside up by shifting the weight of their
bodies, then quickly re-emerging from the other side and
grinning at her with greased, dripping faces.

Asiak smiled at the memory of Ernenek who many years
ago had tried using a kayak, but scorned advice on how to
fasten the jacket watertight to the hatch, and after his
second somersault the kayak was full of water—and so was
Ernenek. But the main reason for the shipwreck, as was
realized later, was that among the scores of assorted charms
he was wearing on his person there wasn't the foot of a
loon which only can assure the skill necessary for han-
dling a kayak. Fortunately there was an umiak in the vicin-
ity, and one of the whalers harpooned Ernenek just in
time, so he was saved from drowning, losing nothing but
a lot of face and blood.

Saved for the bear.

She gazed after the kayakers till they had paddled themselves out of sight. Then she advanced to the edge of the
strip, where the ice was gray and brittle. Under her weight
a pan of ice broke off from the strip and drifted with the
current. She noticed it without having to look back, for
the icepan was slowly revolving and soon she was facing
the village, separated from it by a growing channel. She
pulled her jacket tightly over her chest as if she were cold.

But she was not afraid. Death could not be harder than
life.

Two women spotted her drifting on the floe. "Asiak is
going to her death," said one to the other.

125

"Is she trying to drown herself or is it an accident?"

"Who knows?"

But they made neither move nor sound toward her rescue. Sedna, the good Queen of the Sea, who provided all the good fish and seal, was well entitled to a catch of her own once in a while, and if she saw herself robbed of it she might take vengeance on the interferers, withholding her products from them and their families.

Asiak looked into the water that surrounded her and wondered how it would feel. Her body had never come in touch with it. The surface spangled under the steel-gray sky and she discerned fish floating and darting, darting and floating in the dark depths.

The good, warm water! The good, fat fish!

A puppy that Papik had left behind had followed her unnoticed. Its downy tail curled up, its heavy brow puckered over its slant eyes, it looked alternately at Asiak and the unfamiliar waters with quick tiltings of its furry head.

She noticed it only after she had jumped in, coming back gasping to the surface. Her clothes were growing heavy as rock, her ears and nostrils filled with water, and the alien taste of salt stabbed her throat. The pup had plunged after her and paddled desperately in her direction, scratching her face with its young unblunted nails, and for an instant she held on to it instinctively. Then she let go of it, bubbling, "Go, go. . . ."

But the pup wouldn't have known where to go even if it had understood her words.

CHAPTER TEN

The Seed

KOHARTOK, the white preacher, had a bell which he clanged with all his might when he saw in his book that it was Sunday.

He was the only person who had remained on shore after darkness and frost had closed in on the cove. Everyone else had built igloos over the water, for the land had grown too cold and it would have required more fuel than was available to warm the huts of stones and sod; but they had built their new dwellings close to the beach and the wood cabin where Kohartok lived.

No sooner had the explorers departed when he had nailed on the door a sign bearing the word MISSION, though he was the only one who could read. They had left him, besides some of their provisions which were too cumbrous to carry, also several cases filled with instruments and books containing their observations and which were to be shipped back on the steamboat. The explorers were not coming back to the village, but would dismiss their guides after traversing the big icecap beyond which were other white men and ships that would take them back to their own people.

Kohartok had also sizable supplies of his own, provided by white men and women of good will way below the horizon, where the sun comes from, to help him spread the Seed among the heathen. He had bridled his missionary zeal so long as he shared the cabin with the other white men. When they had gone, he swung into action with daily sessions to which were summoned one and all. Colored pictures backed up his readings from a simplified version of the Holy Scripture, prepared by the Mission that sponsored him.

Since he knew that in order to make people Christians it was necessary first to convince them they were sinners, he used the beginning of winter to instill into his audience a consciousness of sin and the wickedness of human nature of which they seemed entirely unaware, stressing their need of salvation until they began to suspect they were doomed.

But bearing in mind that good preachers give fruits rather than flowers he always concluded his sessions with handouts of sugared tea and canned keks. Naterk, a woman old enough to be set out on the ice, played hostess and kept house for him.

With sufficient stored provisions to draw from and no reason to worry, with no chance for gossip due to the absence of men, any diversion was a rare treat, and nobody would have missed even one of Kohartok's sessions, which were interesting as well as profitable.

Between the preacher and the angakok a gentleman's agreement had been established. Siorakidsok might continue curing sickness in his own fashion, to influence the weather and the hunting season, so long as he did not interfere with Kohartok's missionary activity. The old angakok had even pledged himself to endorse the new Faith, provided the preacher would impress upon his flock that setting toothless old men out on the ice was a grave sin—a condition which Kohartok had no difficulty in accepting, thus convincing Siorakidsok that the Christian was an upstanding, commendable religion indeed.

An arrant glutton, he was the first to arrive at the sessions, carried by his granddaughters, Torngek and Neghe; when the session was over they woke him, and after he had scooped up the last crumb and cleaned the sugar bowl he tarried to converse with the white man over various matters approaching profundity.

In some communities overzealous missionaries clashed

with the local angakoks. But Kohartok was mild as the moon and Siorakidsok wise enough to leave alone those who left him alone. It was all the same to either of them whether a gash was treated with iodine or rabbit dung, since both treatments proved successful. And in the face of graver developments the two men were equally helpless. So the white ship of Christian Faith had smooth sailing in the little cove, unruffled by worries or distractions.

At first.

A woman had stunned a wolverine with a lucky stone throw during its mating, tied its paws and jaws, and called the village for a feast. They had torn off the beast's claws one at a time, pulled out its tongue, stuck sewing needles into its bladder, then cut out the ripe, crawling litter from its pregnant belly and gone to work on them, forgetting about the mother.

Kohartok, attracted by the clamor, had grown very angry.

But that was nothing compared to his anger on hearing that a mother had taken her latest-born girl to the grave-yard and left her there naked to freeze quickly.

Kohartok had no easy task. While the Eskimo vocabulary could boast several words for the Devil it lacked a word for God; so the Mission had to invent one which roughly meant Top Spirit, and Kohartok sweated trying to explain the concept of Him. But his difficulties did not end there. Even though, under the double-barreled promise of rewards in Heaven and punishments in Hell, Eskimos had always proved easy to convert (who were they to doubt a member of the powerful race that produced steel knives, Primus stoves, firearms, and firewater?) yet many traditions were too deeply ingrained to be shunned overnight, even if it was an Arctic night, and the new doctrine often had to share honors with ancient habits.

So the Eskimos were surprised that Kohartok didn't

participate in their hatred of the wolverine; that he de-
nounced the practice of killing the new-born and the aged
only because the supporting capacity of the land was lim-
ited; that he frowned on nakedness, no matter how hot it
was; and on the habit of overeating when meat was abundant, just to make up for the ever-recurring times of dearth.

But what caused special alarm from the start was his
attitude toward sex.

After his first distribution of refreshments following his
arrival a delegation of husbands had offered him the pick
of their wives, to show their gratitude. Surely a man who
had come a long way without the comfort of women
should be in the mood for a little laughter. But it appeared
that if he ever was in a mood for it he laughed by himself,
for he grew incensed at the proposition and red in the
face, chasing the delegation indignantly from the house,
amid the uproarious hilarity of the explorers. The incident
provided a welcome opening for his campaign against
adultery, promiscuity, wife-trading, and what other forms
of sinfulness the villagers' activity was wont to assume.

Heretofore they had been taught to regard as sinful the
slaying of a white caribou, for women to hunt seal and
whale or to sew out of season, and countless other deeds,
none of which, however, concerned sex, and the new taboos introduced by the white man jeopardized some of
their fondest habits, while for the first time the thought
of it began to occupy and preoccupy their minds.

The favorite target of Kohartok's wrath was Torngek.
Although informed of the wickedness of bigamy she hadn't
promised to dismiss one and properly marry the other of
her mates upon their return. Women, she alleged, were
scarce; she was fond of both her husbands, and both
needed her. So she was not considered fit for baptism.

But her sister Neghe welcomed the idea of monogamy
which would reserve for her all of Argo's attentions.

Kohartok was a conscientious man and was cautious

with baptisms, knowing that many Eskimos took up the new Faith just as a fad, or to be polite to the friendly stranger; and in some advanced communities because they hoped it might get them better rates at the trading post— as it frequently did.

He had performed only one baptism before the expedition's departure, that of Alinaluk, an old woman, and mainly because she was at the point of death. She had died of gangrene, despite Siorakidsok's exorcisms and dung treatments. In the winter he baptized first Papik's fancy, Vivi, and her mother Padlock; then the other women and children, including his housekeeper, Naterk, about whom he was not sure save for the fact that she was outside the scope of sinful activity due to her advanced age; everybody in fact, except Torngek and Siorakidsok.

Siorakidsok had asked to be converted but, admittedly, as a token of his friendship only, which wasn't a satisfactory reason for the preacher, and the angakok received this shouted information with unconcealed relief.

Small children could be baptized without hesitation, and when in the dark of the night a girl was born to Neghe, she became the community's first Christian baby. In the choice of her name the native custom was observed of using that of a deceased person. As Asiak's name had already been given to a lovely husky pup that would keep it warm and comfortable, the little girl was christened Ernenek, and Ivaloo was happy that her father's name had ceased to drift lonesome in the cold night and found a body to harbor in.

Water was sprinkled, salt was strewn, sermons delivered, prayers offered, hymns sung, and the village got tea and keks.

Other babies were born after Neghe's. Before departing, the men had planted their seed in the good earth of woman's womb and in their absence it budded, grew, yielded fruit. Torngek, the last expectant mother, was delivered of twins, and the whole village had a belly laugh, saying she got twins because she had two husbands. Kohartok frowned at their jests but beamed at the christening for he had snatched two more souls from the eternal fire.

No new babies would be forthcoming for a long time.

Among the flat, large-mouthed, almond-eyed faces lined up on the wood benches to receive reverently the Good Word, Kohartok noticed one above all others. It was the attentive, rapt face of a girl sitting spraddle-legged in boots of ringed seal extending to the crotch.

There was nothing decadent in her way of dressing. Next to tall and slender Vivi, who appeared to be her contemporary and with whom she kept company, she looked chubby in the Northern clothes of young bearhide which seemed exceedingly rough next to the suits of caribou or of white and blue fox, carefully patterned and trimmed with ermine and little shells, worn by the other women; but she was straight and well built, childbearing having not yet broadened her back. And, while the other women wore their hair flat on top and parted in the middle in two long tresses, she wore hers gathered high up on her head and fastened with fishbones in a turret-like knot that bobbed when she walked, in the fashion of the Polar women. The hair's blue-black color and her dark irises made her old-ivory complexion and the new ivory of her teeth the more conspicuous.

She should have smiled more often.

Once, after the others had left, Kohartok sat on a bench with her and took her hands into his. Her eyes widened at the touch. The hands of all white men were inordinately large, but it was the first time she had touched one, and was surprised to find it very agile and weak, and soft as of a new-born babe—a hand that had never gripped a spear nor wielded a whip.

"What is your name, Sister?" he asked warmly.

"Ivaloo."

"What a beautiful name—the name of the first woman God made from the first man's rib!"

"Yes, and somebody was very happy to hear that!"

"Have you been listening to all lessons as attentively as to the first, Sister?"

Ivaloo nodded forcefully.

"Are you conscious of the fact that your soul will live on in the Hereafter?"

"A girl has always been very conscious of it, Kohartok, because her mother used to tell her so."

"And are you ready to be saved?"

"Saved from what? Nobody wants to do somebody any harm. Everyone is very good to a young girl."

"Saved from yourself! It is within you that the real danger lurks."

"What do you mean, Kohartok? Somebody is just a stupid girl."

"God loves the simple of mind, Ivaloo. Remember: 'Blessed are the pure in heart, for they shall see God.'"

"Shall somebody really see Him?"

"Of course you will—if you are ready to surrender your life to Him. Are you, Ivaloo?"

"Aren't all our lives in His hands?"

"Indeed they are! But are you willing to disclose your heart to Him?"

"Can't He peer into our darkest corners?"

"Are you ready or not," Kohartok cried with a touch of impatience, "to make peace with your Maker?"

Ivaloo blushed and lowered her eyes. "Have we been wrangling?"

Kohartok, himself a man of faith, knew how to discriminate between sheep and goats, and so he recognized what glowed deep in Ivaloo's heart, illuminating her face, as the real thing, and no doubt about it.

And there were many other true believers besides Ivaloo.

Was it that unusual life devoid of menfolk which made the women particularly receptive to the Seed? Be that as it may, the Seed was bearing fruit, and they prayed and believed with the candor of children and the fervor of novices.

They adored their preacher. He was a kind man, busy always doing good works. When his old Naterk fell ill with pains in her abdomen he looked after her more than she could look after him, recoiling only slightly before the lice swarming on her thinning hair and mangy clothes, and wondering meanwhile who might take her place.

He consulted Siorakidsok.

Siorakidsok had two suggestions. First, that though it was meet to provide for old men, especially maimed angakoks, doing the same for any old hag meant carrying things too far, so the best thing would be to strip Naterk of her clothes, fill her toothless mouth with snow, and expose her in the night for her final slumber, thus putting her out of her misery and saving the community considerable bother. His second proposition was to entrust Ivaloo with Naterk's housekeeper duties. She was a strong, industrious and willing wench who might be able to toil thrice as hard as Naterk ever had.

Kohartok scouted the first suggestion as readily as he accepted the second. Ivaloo was overjoyed. Not only was it an honor serving the white man, but the fact that she might assist him in his missionary activity made her heart overflow with happiness. It also established her authority with the fellow-natives, though she was unaware of it. Being entrusted with the key to the Mission's pantry would be anyone's dream.

Anyone's, alas, but Ivaloo's, who had not yet developed a sweet tooth.

As Naterk's pains increased, the preacher said to Siorakidsok:

"Maybe you can do something to relieve her suffering."

"What can a powerless angakok do? But surely a white man knows how to chase the evil spirits that have entered her."

"I may be able to drive the devil from her heart but not the pains from her body," Kohartok avowed frankly. "But your remedies sometimes give surprising results."

Siorakidsok hemmed and hawed for a long stretch, slighting his ability, before declaring himself ready to try.

"However, to know exactly what treatment the old hag requires, an angakok must first consult with the Moon Spirit."

"Do what you want, so long as you help her."

Siorakidsok asked to be taken into the hills from where he would start on one of the hazardous journeys to the moon that all angakoks undertake when circumstances require it. But since the terrible-tempered Moon Spirit is likely to be difficult with petitioners he refused to leave without bearing a load of fanciful viands as a gift.

A little snowhouse filled with hides was erected in a secluded spot—a comfortable snowhouse being an indispensable starting point for a journey to the moon—and Siorakidsok was left there alone with bucketfuls of such delicacies as boiled whale and walrus hide, raw intestines of fish, and a mellow mixture of chewed salmon, shad roe and seal oil, and nobody was permitted to approach the spot while the angakok was on his trip under penalty of immediate and horrible death.

Three sleeps later the village, including Kohartok, went to fetch him back. They found him dozing, obviously exhausted from the perilous journey. The food buckets were empty, which was a good sign.

He had learned from the Moon Spirit that the demon which caused Naterk's illness housed in her right breast, into which he made an incision. As she didn't improve in spite of this, Siorakidsok opened a hole in her belly to allow the pains to escape, then slaughtered a litter of lemmings and laid their hot skins over the wound.

Naterk was the second villager to be buried in the Christian cemetery a short time later, after an impressive ceremony and a ringing sermon.

Ivaloo did Naterk's work so well that Kohartok wondered how he had ever got along without her.

She liked her duties but suffered from excessive warmth in the house of wood heated by a coal stove, and more so in her periods of rest than when she was about, absorbed by her duties. She slept on a cot in the room Naterk had used, which seemed to her a most luxurious living place, although it was nothing but a cubicle partitioned off from the main room where the preacher slept by the stove. He shunned the cold like the devil, never allowed the windows to be opened, and when upon rising he set the water bucket onto the fire to melt the ice, Ivaloo saw him shiver.

He was kind to her. The explorers had left him a few bottles of firewater that he kept in case of sudden illness, and when he saw her cry, because she felt lonely, he let her have a little, mixed with snow, after taking some himself to show it didn't hurt.

Ivaloo could fall asleep half frozen, and like it, but she would never learn to sleep when it was too warm, and upon retiring she would take off all her clothes. Asked whether this was a sin, the startled preacher had answered, No, it isn't—when one is alone and all is dark; but running around the house naked in broad daylight should be avoided. So lying in the dark in the warm room, Ivaloo experienced for the first time the feel of her own flesh, and her small hard palms, advancing warily into the unexplored territory of her body, were startled at the smoothness of its skin.

After exploring her body she sometimes ventured to muse over the future, yet, unable to pierce the veil that shrouded it, she reverted to the past that was clear in her mind: gay, exciting, and already beautified by time. So beautiful that it swelled her heart with sadness and her eyes with tears. How she yearned for the path of the bear track and the long crouching over the fish holes and the runs over the windswept sea fields and the hasty shelter building in the howling blizzard! How lonesome she was for the quaint atmosphere of the igloo, the rich smell of burning blubber mingling with the sweet odor of wasting meats, the sunset glow of the wick on the circular wall, the sound of Asiak's scraping and stitching and her quiet remarks, of Ernenek's snoring and laughter!

Thinking of the lost paradise filled her with such sadness that she sought comfort in the paradise to come, and spoke to God on that behalf. And while speaking to Him, Ivaloo had the feeling He lent her an attentive Ear. But she had no proof. That was her own fault, had said Kohartok, whose breathing came from the adjoining room deep and regular, proving that he was beset by no such doubts.

"Will He ever come to such a stupid girl?" she had once asked him.

"He will, if you have enough faith. Just pray, and believe. Or have you forgotten what the Good Book says? 'And all things, whatsoever you shall ask in prayer, believing, you shall receive.'"

"But how shall a girl know when He comes?"

"You will know. If you are not certain, He hasn't come."

So it was obvious that He hadn't come, and she worried about it. It kept her awake too long, too often. She besought Him to manifest Himself to her. Maybe in one of her dreams. Or to touch her hand. Only once. She would be content with that.

She visualized Him in human form, as He had made man in His image, yet she had sense enough to realize He wasn't at the immediate disposal of any little girl that wished to see Him, but that He was a Busy One, doubtless with heavier sinners to worry about than she was.

So she braced herself with patience and prayed and waited that He should find time for her.

Occasionally she thought she heard a Voice in the gale, sensed a Finger in the draft that played on her shoulder as she lay there naked in the dark. But these signs weren't positive enough, so that couldn't be it. And she was right.

For the time He finally came to her there was no doubt left in anyone.

CHAPTER ELEVEN

The Fruit

IT WAS Torngek, credited with considerable experience, owing to her reprehensible state of bigamy, who was the first to commit herself to a definite statement as to Ivaloo's condition. This was not, as the ignorant girl thought, due to something she had eaten, even though of late her appetite had noticeably increased.

The real reason for Ivaloo's spreading was pregnancy.

And that her pregnancy was a miracle was as evident as the molehill growing on the white plains of her belly, and all the women gathered to see it with their own eyes and touch it with their own hands.

The stars had faded, a purple glow circled the horizon— half a year had passed since the expedition had left with every male capable of such a deed. The oldest boy of the village was about eight; after him came Siorakidsok, and that he was out of the race had been ascertained by the women longer ago than he cared to remember. Only Kohartok was in the age of manhood but, being a preacher, he was of course excluded from any such activities.

Moreover, Ivaloo would know if she had laughed with a man, and no girl had ever been more positive that she had stayed serious.

She wondered whether just thinking of men, or being looked at the way Milak had looked at her, sufficed to put a girl that way; but the more experienced women ruled it out.

"However," said Torngek, "the full moon may render a girl pregnant."

"Yes," said Neghe. "Have you ever stood outdoors gazing at the full moon? Or did you ever drink water on which the full moon was shining?"

"No, never! Mother didn't allow it. She said married women, only, may do that."

"In that case it can only be God's child," said Vivi's mother, Padlock, with finality; she was very religious and had refused to accompany her husband on the expedition in order not to miss Sunday services.

"It must be," Torngek whispered, clapping her hands and smiling entrancedly.

Ivaloo wore an expression of bliss that was not of this earth. "Somebody thinks to know when it happened," she said, and although she spoke with but a thread of a voice, the spellbound circle didn't miss a word.

"A girl was very sad once while preparing to retire, feeling more lonesome than ever for all the departed ones. The preacher, seeing me cry, read the sentence from the Good Book that says: 'Blessed are they that mourn, for they shall be comforted,' and gave somebody a little of his precious firewater that, like prayer, is a potent medicine and a source of comfort. But in bed a young girl felt lonelier than ever and very hot with firewater, and cried very loud, till weakness and giddiness came from the many tears. Then she received a visit."

"Who was it?" the women chorused, for Ivaloo had stopped, reminiscing.

"For a long time somebody had been praying for God to visit her during her rest. And that time He finally did."

"You actually saw Him?"

"Not with my eyes, for it was dark. But somebody felt Him."

"You touched Him?"

"No: He touched somebody. Suddenly large soft hands sweep her tears away and glide over her body, and she feels like weeping some more, not out of fright but because a great warmth and tenderness overcome her as if all the things and people she ever loved were in those hands."

"But was it real or were you dreaming?" asked Neghe.

"Somebody doesn't know. At the time she thought it was just a dream, and was glad that God had at last manifested Himself in it. But now a girl thinks it was real and it only felt like a dream because she was dizzy from too much crying, and very limp from the firewater. Somebody's head hurt a little upon awakening, and so did her groin."

"Oh Ivaloo, little one," said Padlock softly, ecstasy on her face. "This is a great hour indeed. Let us tell Kohartok!"

And they rushed out in a body to the Mission.

But the preacher did not receive the glad tidings with the enthusiasm they had anticipated. He seemed indeed impressed, actually shaken, for he turned pale and his blue eyes fluttered like those of a stricken ptarmigan, but his face showed no ecstasy, no cry of joy issued irrepressibly from his throat, no thanksgiving soared to Heaven from the depths of his heart, no sermon, no hymn, no prayer went to glorify the miraculous annunciation. He just stood thunderstruck, rooted to the ground.

"It came to pass that you were right," Ivaloo told him, bending her head in humility. "A girl's faith has borne fruit."

Thus the rocky torrents of doubt and sorrow that had been in Ivaloo came to a stop, overflowing to a deep quiet pool. Her vivacious eyes grew slow and serene, and a sense of mellowness and contentment suffused her with a deep and glowing warmth—a warmth that no longer kept her awake but brought balm and distension to the most intimate cords of her being.

She began to crave solitude while her body and soul seemed to converge to the molehill growing from out of the dark and that came to mean center, beginning and end of the universe. It divested all else of importance. The death of her parents had lost its sting. The return of Papik and Milak was urgent no longer. Whether it was winter or summer, whether she was North or South, whether the seal surfaced or the musk ox calved, what matter? All that mattered was the new life stirring and kicking so boldly within her that at times the women could see her belly move and she had to hold it still with both hands amid the general merriment.

Kohartok took Tippo, a much older woman, into the house to help with the chores, on the grounds that Ivaloo had to husband her strength since she was with child, even if she didn't consider her duties any strain or bother. Tippo was happy to come and Ivaloo didn't mind too much sharing her cubbyhole. She didn't mind anything.

Kohartok gave slow but sure signs of being affected by the event. Deepening lines appeared on his brow. He seemed tired, and yet restless, and somehow older. His sermons grew more earnest, his prayers longer, his assistance to the aged and sick more extensive.

A deep seriousness and passion pervaded the flock. With their shepherd in the lead they wallowed in self-accusations. Even Ivaloo, not to be outdone, acknowledged gladly that she was a frightful sinner. Yet everyone looked upon her with envy and with awe. Without being mellow, her singing voice was clear and resonant, soaring high above the chorus in the delivery of the beautiful Christian hymns that had supplanted the disreputable native ballads.

"*False and full of sin I am,*" led Kohartok's mournful

bass, and the congregation echoed happily in a variety of keys:

"*False and full of sin I am. . . .*"

Time made a mountain out of the molehill. Spring came and, owing to the continuous daylight, the scant snow melted and the dwarf vegetation sprouted swiftly, and in but a few weeks the brown earth, rich with the manure of the million birds, was covered with yellow poppies, vari-colored saxifrage, Arctic willow and flimsy birches entirely recumbent on the ground, while red and mauve niviarsiak clustered on the rocks and tiny ferns carpeted the humid ravines. Once more the huge icebergs, released from frost, drifted southward with the current, the swift kayaks cut capers in the water, spangling with sunshine among the floes, the women dug traps and set snares, the boys fished, raided the auk nests on the cliffs and put their blotched eggs to rot in the sun, or caught the clumsy ptarmigans with their bare hands, while the girls gathered the mani-fold berries that grew in the bushes, all very savory when mixed with oil and easy to preserve for the wintertide when frozen in blubber.

Seal and walrus, narwhal and white whale were afloat in the liquid ocean, and if anyone had been available to man the umiaks there would have been orgies of fresh blood and clams and oysters from their stomachs and mattak from their skins, but no woman might harpoon a seal or a whale lest all sealdom and whalekind, mortally offended by such an insult, should decide to withdraw to the bottom of the ocean and never allow themselves to be caught again. And the boys were too little to catch anything but small fish, and an occasional seal cub that had not yet learned to swim, bloodless, white of skin, and empty of stomach.

In the height of summer a smoking-boat steamed into the little cove.

It was a great day. New faces, new voices, new foods. Moreover, the white sailors brought the good news that the expedition had reached its destination, which meant the men were coming home.

This ship didn't carry any regular traders, but every man from the captain to the stoker was an amateur trader, eager to do business. They had brought along mirrors and scissors and beads and bottles and knives and ribbons that they bartered for oil and hides. They were great, gruff, hirsute fellows who smiled seldom but made a lot of noise. They organized wild dances to the tune of their music boxes, and after drinking firewater they acted as if demented, growing obnoxiously loud, offensively rough, and setting hard after the women, even the old toothless ones, as if they had never heard speak of sin and hot seats in Hell. Some sailors became so troublesome after too much drink that their mates had to drag them back to the boat, not without difficulty and fights. The natives had never seen such roughness and violence.

Yet few of them would have wanted to miss any of those goings on, for their very oddness and the change they afforded.

The preacher looked on with a frown but said nothing. Not even when for the first time he saw empty spaces on his benches—and there were women who could no longer look him straight in the eye after they had taken a walk with a sailor.

The smoking-boat had come purposely to load the cases left behind by the explorers. The captain, one of the few who chose the rich but dangerous Arctic waters infested by icebergs, was in a hurry to leave again, for summer was short here, the waters open to navigation not longer than a month, and this was the height of the whaling season. His boat was large only to native eyes; actually it was but a small whaling vessel, doing errands on the side, with a crew not quite a dozen strong.

One sleep before it was to weigh anchor, Kohartok again sat with Ivaloo on one of the crude little benches and took her hands into his. He looked pale and haggard, with great blue shadows under his eyes.

"I have decided to go away from here, little one," he said.

"Everybody always leaves!" she said distressed. "Why? Are you tired of spreading the Seed among us?"

He shifted nervously from one side to the other. "There come times even to a preacher when he begins to doubt. Not of Truth, but of himself. And to carry on, I need your help, Ivaloo."

"The help of a stupid girl?"

"What you are going to hear might surprise you, little one: but I wish you would become my wife. Let us be married before God and together carry the Torch through the darkness!"

He had to repeat twice before she trusted her ears. Then she blushed deeply and lowered her eyes.

"If only a stupid girl's parents could have lived the day a white man, and one of your importance, asked her to be his wife! Do you think they see it?"

"It is likely."

"Somebody is honored, Kohartok."

He pensively stroked his reddish beard and said with a sigh, "Don't mention it, little one."

"And it grieves somebody sorely having to refuse your offer."

"You refuse? But why?" he cried, relieved.

"You are not much of a hunter, nor do you know how to handle a team, nor anything about the things a girl likes, except about God. That's why. But now there is a worry on somebody's mind: who will baptize her child if you are gone? And who will conduct services and show us the way to God?"

"I can't teach you anything of the ways of God, Iva-

144

loo. I am just another sinner. You shall carry on in my behalf—with the help of this book. Its pictures will help you teach and remember the Good Story."

He opened his book, took a flower out that had been drying between the leaves—a flower with four large purple petals—and offered it to Ivaloo:

"Take this. It is a flower from my country."

"Delicious!" said Ivaloo, eating it.

Kohartok's departure saddened everyone. He was a fine, good man. He had such kind eyes. He belched so delicately. Yet he took leave in the most obnoxious manner, loudly advertising his departure and looking up every member of the community to shake hands with. So they all escorted him to the boat and waved farewell with tears in their eyes, even those that had miserably failed the Test, deserting School and Chapel since the arrival of the sailors.

It seemed to one and all that he had lost much of his erstwhile harshness toward the end. He didn't scold the sinners in his farewell address; he said only, "As the Good Book has it, 'Watch and pray, that you enter not into temptation: the spirit indeed is willing, but the flesh is weak.'"

A school of kayaks convoyed the boat for a stretch in the watery wake it cut through the floating ice, and the rest of the community, including Siorakidsok, stood on the beach till the smoke from the stack merged with the summer mist.

The news of the smoking-boat's arrival at the cove had spread somehow, as news will, and in no time at all a handful of Netchiliks had come to pitch their tents round the settlement, although the height of summer was the worst season for traveling; but they left after the boat had weighed anchor, and by the time night had closed in again and the villagers had moved into their winter igloos over the water, the community had reverted to normal.

The light from the blubber lamps shone faintly through the walls and the dark cove was dotted with the dim, warm glow from the dome-shaped little snowhouses.

Services went on, conducted by Ivaloo who availed herself of Kohartok's picture book. She couldn't read but knew her illustrations well. She had no means of knowing when it was Sunday and the services were desultory. Whenever she thought the villagers were in need of religion, which happened almost after every sleep and sometimes in between, she clanged the bell for a round of tea and Sisters-let-us-pray. She related the Good Story as well as she knew how, and answered questions the same way.

Old Tippo proved a crusty person whose company Ivaloo avoided, allowing her to sleep in the big room by the stove. The gluttonous old woman spent sleepless nights devising ways and means to get to the sweets that Ivaloo kept out of her reach, for Kohartok had been explicit on how the Mission goods should be administered. Woe betide those natives who in true heathen fashion should presume that the community of goods which they held might apply to Mission stores! Ivaloo husbanded them with the greatest parsimony.

To keep Tippo away from the sugar bowl Ivaloo had asked Vivi to help her with the distribution of tea, and that increased the old glutton's wrath. Vivi was a good friend and easy to joke with, and since Papik had expressed interest in her before his departure, Ivaloo talked often about him, and Vivi didn't seem to mind.

She had experienced pangs before but once she wakened in the midst of sleep knowing this was it. She dressed in a hurry between pangs and chills, in silence lest she wake Tippo, and rushed to Siorakidsok's house.

"You asked to be present when it happened," she told the women there.

One of Torngek's little girls was sent out to notify the other women, and they soon started swarming in.

"Not so loud or you will wake Siorakidsok. A silly girl doesn't want him to watch," Ivaloo said.

Vivi arrived out of breath and very excited and directly began pulling down Ivaloo's pants; but the women laughed.

"Keep off, you stupid girl," said Torngek, giving her a push. "It isn't yet."

Siorakidsok, who had an uncanny ear for everything he wasn't supposed to hear, woke at the noise.

"Please leave the house for a moment," Ivaloo told him. Siorakidsok flew into a rage when he finally understood. "Somebody has seen more children born than you'll have men in your life!"

"Yes, but please leave the house just the same."

A compromise was reached by taking him to the farthest corner, with his face to the wall, fuming, and the women crowded round Ivaloo who lay on the couch with her eyes staring and her face intent, waiting for the pains. When they came her lips twitched and she snorted subduedly. She felt abysmally thirsty but too sick to talk, and she strove to keep quiet lest Siorakidsok, who was snoring again in the far corner, should wake.

The pains quickened and when they came with hardly any respite at all, she said, "Now!" as if she had borne a hundred times before.

Arms helped her from the couch down to the floor, putting her on her knees. Hands pushed her trousers and high boots down a little. Someone dug a hole in the snow beneath her, and Torngek embraced her from behind and pressed her.

"Push!"

Ivaloo felt sweat at the roots of her hair, and drops of it

147

tickled the tip of her nose. The room swam before her eyes. She heard the women shout, "Here comes the head! Push harder. You must help, silly girl. Once the head is out the worst is over." There was a great tearing, and in the deep gloom of pain, where everything went dark before her eyes, she suddenly saw the damp top of the child's head with a crest of wet hair glinting beneath her. Torngek kept pressing, cutting her breath, and the women cheered, and the house bitch, fired by the general excitement, stretched her nose forward, whimpering and sniffing, till she was kicked away. And before Ivaloo was quite aware of it the child had dropped and Torngek's weight came off her back.

Padlock had received the new-born in her hands and as soon as Neghe had cut it free it wailed with all its power. The women slapped a foxskin between Ivaloo's legs, pulled up her pants, and gave her a drink of melted snow.

"Maybe you wish to rest a little before going home?"

"Yes, if you'll excuse a stupid girl for being such bother," Ivaloo said, stretching out on the couch. "Where is the little one?"

Neghe, having wiped and greased the child, wrapped it in a clean skin and handed it to Ivaloo saying:

"It is a boy."

"Please bring a lot of light."

Padlock and Torngek lit two tallow flares and brought them on, and Ivaloo dropped the hide from her son and lifted him up into the light. His wailing tapered off and there was only the sound of the flares crackling and the bitch licking the ground. Then the voice of Siorakidsok awakening:

"Is Ivaloo about to have her child?"

Nobody answered. The women knelt in mute adoration, hands folded, and the bitch came up sniffing, putting her forepaws onto the couch, stretching her nose forward and whimpering in wonderment—for though she was an old and widely traveled bitch and had seen many new-born babes, she had never seen one quite like this.

And an unusually beautiful one it was, with eyes the color of Heaven and hair the color of Hell.

CHAPTER TWELVE

Tetarartee

IVALOO performed the baptism of her son with as much pomp as she could muster, christening him Poopooliluk. She didn't know what the name meant, but she had once heard of a foreign tribesman who was so called, and thought it the most beautiful name ever to flatter her ear. Since then she had always secretly hoped to have a son someday, so she could name him Poopooliluk.

She had never suspected a human being could be so happy as she was now. Conducting services, and being able to baptize her own son! What had she done to deserve all this?

But discipline was lax under Ivaloo's regime. That careless girl forgot to denounce even those running around the house naked or eating beyond hunger, nor is it to be completely excluded that she indulged in some of it herself.

But meanwhile men and women gathered round her to watch and worship her son—not only villagers, but also travelers and pilgrims from afar. The affluence of nomads upon the last call of the smoking-boat at the cove had caused the news of the virgin pregnancy to spread. It was a good yarn to unwind when one's turn of storytelling came at last in an attentive igloo; and so the news had traveled, received with laughter, wonder, incredulity, or belief; yet it had spread in all directions, and mainly south, like the rays of the sun. And sleds sought out the cove in the dark of winter, foreign teams joined their howling at the moon, that came from the wolf blood in their veins, to the howling of the village huskies, while the new-arrived erected igloos in convenient nearness to the Mission.

And when they were come into the house they saw the young child with Ivaloo, his mother, and fell down, and worshiped him; and when they opened their treasures they presented unto him gifts: dolls carved from wood and bone or sewn of cloth and fur, knives with handles of chiseled horn, skillfully sculptured walrus tusks, cow bladders swollen with tea and tobacco, flimsy fabrics bartered from foreign traders, extravagant foods in shining tin cans, and an occasional bottle of firewater.

Some visitors were heathen and some were Christians, converted by other missionaries in other localities, but all listened with equal reverence to the Word as delivered by Ivaloo and joined her in her prayers and her hymns.

Some heathens, having looked and listened, asked to be converted, were sprinkled with water and touched with salt, as Ivaloo had watched Kohartok do it, and went away beaming. Others stayed on—but not all to worship and pray. Some stayed because the village was growing to a large community and they liked the hustle and bustle of sleds arriving and leaving.

Some traders also came. They stepped in to see the virgin and her son, grinned, stepped out again, and started to trade.

The village expanded as the snowhouses mushroomed; Ivaloo found it difficult to accommodate all visitors in the Mission; new benches had to be built of snow and covered with hides, and round the altar on which Poopooliluk lay to be adored the offerings piled up.

A man named Gaba asked to be converted together with his three wives. Ivaloo had seen women who had two, three, or four husbands, especially in the North where women were scarce, but it was the first time she heard of a man with more than one wife. She had never understood why it was wrong having more than one mate at a time, but then taboos were made to be respected, not understood; so she impressed on Gaba that he should send away at least a couple of his wives if he wished to be converted.

Neither was Gaba in the habit of arguing over taboos and showed himself most reasonable.

"A man will gladly send away a couple of wives," he said. "However, he has acquired them just recently, killing their husband, so needs time to decide which one is worth keeping."

Ivaloo scolded him but granted him time to make up his mind, and meanwhile converted him and his following of wives anyway. Gaba was grateful and stayed on, proving a great asset to the community, as any man able to keep three wives should be. Game was far from plentiful in this season nor easy to spot in the dark, but Gaba was a paramount hunter and soon had become the community's leader. This didn't mean he had authority, but he had influence. He planned the hunting forays and directed the men. His reward came when he saw the others eat what he had obtained. Even if he had more than his share of wives he was now making up for it by keeping many others well fed, and expelling him from the community would be only the community's loss, and no punishment for him: he would never be lonesome, with three wives to fall back on.

The fruit of the hunt was always divided in equal shares, but those who had contributed least felt mortified and ate without joy, while those who had contributed most beamed and laughed, and the women had eyes for them only.

But despite Gaba's presence the threat of famine yawned at the village after day had broken. Stocks and caches were at last depleted, the settlement was overpopulated and game grew constantly rarer as wherever men appear, and no betterment was to be expected of the impending spring, which was always the leanest season: when the birds still were underway and the vegetation had not sprouted as yet, the great thaw prevented fishing and sealing on the breaking ocean crust, and the retreat of the ice entailed the retreat of bear.

As food was scarce and the outlook worse, many men began to pack their sleds and went away while the frozen ocean permitted traveling. Gaba also left, and proved he meant to keep his promise of cutting down on the number of his wives by leaving behind, hungry, brokenhearted, and almost unclad, the oldest of the trio.

The handful of men who stayed on were not the best: mainly such as didn't even have dogs and sleds of their own. Nor were the women much to boast about. Except for Vivi and Ivaloo, they were all old or ugly, and some were both, since the better-looking ones had decided to go off with the pilgrims toward richer hunting grounds without waiting for the return of their men.

All the old were seriously worried, and so that the others might share in their fears they dug out from the caches of their memories the horror tales from the times of dearth—when fish and seal decide to keep to the bottom of the sea, when bear go on distant hunting trips, when musk ox and caribou and small game vanish as mysteriously as they come, and men and women eat up their dogs and skin boats and meat sleds and sleeping bags, then their dead, and finally those that are not yet dead.

But it was Siorakidsok who was concerned above all others about the situation. He was responsible for the community's well-being and if he didn't provide he might be branded an impostor and treated like any useless old man, now that Kohartok was no longer present to protect him.

When the first sunbeams struck the bay, starting the most critical period, and he noticed that ever more people whispered in his presence, he assembled the community for an urgent message.

"There is a sinner in your midst," he announced menacingly, casting baleful glances in all directions, and there seemed to be nobody who didn't shiver or cringe or quail. "Most likely some woman has tried to kill a seal, or has cooked fish and meat in one and the same pot, or has done even worse than that. It's always the women who commit breaches and the men who must suffer for them!"

Absolute silence followed and Siorakidsok went on petulantly:

"You know full well that just as the mere breaking of a taboo brings trouble on all, so does the public confession of the breach stop it. Why then are you always so reluctant to confess, you ugly bunch of sinners?"

Still no one answered, and Siorakidsok made gestures of despair and heaved several mighty sighs before continuing:

"An angakok shall once more allow himself to be bothered with a journey to the moon in order to learn the name of the culprit. Woe betide her upon one's return! She shall be driven from the village and starve to death by herself, without dragging everyone else into her well-deserved ruin! Therefore start immediately preparing the gifts for the Moon Spirit, everybody! Prepare the dishes with love and care, and use what sweetmeats are left in your larders. This is no time for stinginess!"

"Wait," said Ivaloo. "If an impertinent girl may contradict such an intelligent man, there is not the slightest reason for concern. Nobody will starve."

"Why not?"

"Because God will provide for us all, if only we'll pray and believe. Or haven't you listened to the Good Word? Maybe a lazy girl hasn't shouted it loud enough to penetrate your wise ears?"

Siorakidsok had been noncommittal about the miracle. But now that Ivaloo interfered with his traveling plans he flushed with anger and asked to talk to her alone.

"A man doesn't know whether your God will provide food or not," he said in a low tone of voice as soon as they were by themselves, "but he knows for sure that the ill-natured Moon Spirit, who is already looking forward to our gifts, will take bitter vengeance on you and your son if you interfere with an angakok's journey."

This possibility had never occurred to Ivaloo. The thought that Poopooliluk might be in danger stopped at once her objections, and she helped prepare the gifts for the Moon Spirit with what little delicacies were left in the community—yet none but very mellow dishes, thoroughly masticated by the women, because the Moon Spirit is a very old man and has no teeth.

Even while Siorakidsok was underway there came an invasion of caribou—an uncommon event for the settlement, which was situated beyond the northernmost verge of caribou migration, yet possible in springtime, before day has definitely risen, and darkness and light have alternated at each turn of the sun; then the surface snow that covers the lichen and moss, after melting under the sunrays, may stiffen with a return of frost, preventing the herds from scraping through the crust, and they swarm wildly in all directions in search of forage.

And one herd swarmed to the cove where Ivaloo was Queen and Poopooliluk was King.

Caribou, good and docile, are very fond of people. So they die willingly, in a variety of fashions: allowing themselves to be slain with spears and arrows, to be hocked with knives, or to be caught in pitfalls baited with urine, the salt content of which appeals to them. And while for several turns of the sun men, women and children ate till they were bursting at the seams Ivaloo's prestige soared to unprecedented heights. But she was saddened that the flock had ever doubted.

When Siorakidsok returned from his journey he announced it was he who had persuaded the Moon Spirit to forgive the villagers their sins, as a rare exception, and to dispatch caribou from the South. So the village never knew whether the Christian God or the Moon Spirit deserved the credit, and allowed both parties the benefit of the doubt.

Shortly after the community had taken up their summer residence on the shore, another smoking-boat, plowing a path across the breaking ice, cast anchor in the cove, landing the usual sailors and a new preacher.

He was older than Kohartok and very skinny, which set the natives back a little, till they learned it was due to voluntary fasting, which was healthy for a Christian body and meritorious for a Christian soul; after which they respected his skinniness. He was a tall man with sharp bones about his long dark face, a narrow beaky nose, a high forehead beneath which glittered fiery little eyes. His black hair with threads of white was thinning but he made up for it with a straight beard reaching to his belt.

Although he didn't know more Eskimo words than Kohartok he used them so deftly, and with such authority, that it didn't take the most obtuse listener long to understand what he wanted and didn't want.

And the first thing he didn't want was Ivaloo.

She stood with the others on the beach, smiling at the sight of the ship, with her son strapped to her back.

"Who is in charge of the Mission house?" the white man asked, stepping off the gangway.

Ivaloo came forward.

"Show me the way," he said briskly.

She went ahead while Poopooliluk in the trundle hood craned his neck at the stranger. She opened the Mission door and let the white man in. He waved off those that had thronged after him, including Tippo, and shut the door in their faces.

Ivaloo showed him through the place, pointing out the altar piled high with the gifts of the devout, the cubicle with the colored pictures stuck on the wall over her sleeping cot.

The white man sat down in the chair. His lips were a thin line as he fixed her with lowering eyes.

"Are you the girl named Ivaloo?"

"Yes," she smiled, pleased and surprised that he should know her name.

He silently stroked his whiskers and kept his burning eyes on her.

"You must hand me the key and leave this place," he said.

She gazed at him, baffled. Then she went to the table and slowly picked up her book.

"What have you there?" he asked.

"Our preacher, Kohartok, gave it to somebody before he left."

"I am the preacher now. What for did he give it to you?"

"He said it would help a girl spread the Good Word."

"You have been doing *what?*"

Ivaloo smiled. "A worthless girl has been teaching about God and Jesus, telling the Good Story and showing the pictures. Then we all pray and sing."

The preacher stared speechlessly. She took it as a sign of encouragement. "There are many people who heard the Good Story in this room and as a consequence became Christians."

"And it was probably you who converted them?"

"It is not impossible," said Ivaloo with a smile. He gave a short laugh, and she added quickly, "It wasn't at all difficult. It wasn't so much a stupid girl's words as because of him." She thumbed toward the boy at her back who was peering over her shoulder.

"I have heard of this child of yours," the preacher said darkly, "and that is why I came."

"Indeed?" She was radiant with gratification. "Many people have come from far to worship him but you have come farthest. It is a great honor—like the Wise Men of the East coming for the Infant Jesus," she said fervently, lowering her eyes.

"It is time for you to stop this wicked deception," the white man cried, as if he had used great restraint till then and lost it all at once. "You are speaking blasphemy!"

Her heart gave a plunge. It looked as if this man hadn't come to worship Poopooliluk after all.

"Excuse a stupid girl for failing to understand. What is on your mind?"

"The alleged virgin birth of your child!"

She looked flabbergasted. "Why don't you inquire, white man? Everyone knows it is so."

"My idea," he said in a conciliatory tone, regaining his self-control, "is that the whole matter started when you found yourself pregnant and wouldn't admit having had any doings with a man."

"Why shouldn't a girl admit it?"

"For fear your parents might scold you."

"Somebody has no parents to scold her, alas. But if they were alive they wouldn't scold her, but be glad she has a child. And surely a girl's mother wouldn't have jumped into the water if she had known."

"So your mother committed suicide!" He got up, his eyes widening like those of someone who has just made a great discovery. "And your father was a murderer, probably?"

"He killed only one man," said Ivaloo.

The preacher clapped his hands. "Your father a murderer, your mother a suicide! How could they help raising a wicked liar? 'A corrupt tree cannot bring forth good fruit,' says the Good Book. You poor girl! You are not alone to blame for your wickedness." Here was indeed a soul worth saving. He began pacing the floor. "So that's where your sinfulness comes from, you offspring of an evil-minded couple! For them we can do nothing. But for you we are still in time." He faced her squarely. "I can show you the right path, but it is you who must move your feet."

"Gladly! But you really think a girl's parents are forever damned?" she asked, worried. "Kohartok didn't seem to think so."

"Let us not talk about my predecessor! What do you think?" The dawn of a new victory loomed in sight. "Can you doubt whether your parents are roasting for their sins? And that you had better repent of yours quickly, unless you want to join them?"

"But somebody does want to join them," Ivaloo said firmly. "A girl wouldn't consent to go anywhere but where they are—wherever they are."

The preacher was nonplussed, but rallied quickly. "If you make peace with God, He may yet listen to your prayers and receive their souls, as He will receive yours if you now tell the truth. Did you make up the story for fear that no man would marry you, knowing you were with child? Answer!"

Ivaloo frowned. She couldn't for the life of her understand what he was driving at. "Many men would take me for their wife because women are scarce, and they would be especially happy to take one who already has a male child, thus saving a lot of time and bother."

"Look, girl. Everybody may make mistakes. They become real sins only if you try to cover them up by deception. Each child is the will of God. But you can't go around saying it was He in person who made it. It is not possible! A child is the result of a man and a woman coming together. There is no other way!"

"You mean . . . you don't *believe?*" She stared at him in terror. "You don't believe in the Good Story?"

"It is your story I don't believe!" he cried, red-faced. "You discovered lies can be very convenient, seeing gifts pile up and people worshipping you. But you have committed grave sins and the punishment shall be commensurate. Each time you gave a lesson you committed blasphemy, each time you performed a baptism you committed sacrilege!"

"You sound like a very wise man," Ivaloo said reverently though alarmed, "because somebody doesn't understand a word you are saying."

"I am saying that you had no right to teach the Good Story and no right to conduct services!"

"But Kohartok said a girl might."

"And I say you may not! The conversions you performed are worthless! The baptisms were just mockery!"

"This is very confusing. Then Poopooliluk is not baptized?" she asked dismayed.

"Of course not! Listen, Ivaloo," he said with a change of tone, striving for control. "A large organization has sent me a long way to persuade you to tell the truth. No harm shall come to you if you do. But you must name the father of your child and, if we can catch him, we'll make him marry you, and soon the whole foolish affair will be forgotten."

"How can somebody forget it?"

"You are young and will get over it. And if you fear the women will mock you for your disgrace, I'll take you where no one knows you."

"Why should the women mock a girl? And why should it be a disgrace to have a child? You said it is always the will of God."

"Not the way you begot it!"

"Isn't there only one way of begetting a child? That is,"

159

she quickly corrected herself, smiling, "unless God puts His Finger on you."

"He didn't put His Finger on you!" the preacher thundered. He took a few quick steps forward as if to lay a hand on her, and she recoiled sharply. "Now listen closely, Ivaloo. Maybe you didn't realize, in your youthful stupidity, the gravity of your lie. But now I want a straight answer." His eyes were all knives and arrows, digging furrows in her brow. "With whom did you consummate your sin?"

Ivaloo's eyes swelled with tears. She was afraid of this man who spoke in riddles and seemed possessed. He was probably insane. Likely as not his mother had been bitten by a wolverine while carrying him. She wanted her son in her arms. She loosened the straps under her breast, reached over her shoulder, pulled the little heathen out of her jacket and pressed him to her bosom. But she pressed too hard; he started crying, and she pulled out a rich flowing breast, with fine veins pointing to the black nipple.

The preacher's anger waxed hot. "You are not to do that," he lashed out, stamping the floor.

"He is hungry. . . ."

"But not in front of other people!"

Puzzled, she slipped the breast back into her jacket, while Poopooliluk screamed in rising and sinking tones, outraged.

"Now leave, Ivaloo, and don't come back till you have taken better counsel—and remember that you will have only your own folly to blame if you suffer!"

No one within a short way of the sun had fallen so fast or so deep as Ivaloo.

The new preacher clanged the bell and gathered the community. He didn't seem interested in the white men who had arrived with him on the smoking-boat, nor they in him. His address was in Eskimo language only, and to make sure that every native was present he sent out messengers to pull the snorers out of their bags and call the traders and hunters and trappers and kayakers and whalers in; all except Ivaloo, who had repaired to Siorakidsok's house, and the angakok himself.

Since he was seen scribbling in a book before starting his sermon, and since white men's names are nothing but rude and unpronounceable grunts to the Eskimos, they quickly christened him Tetarartee, or He-Who-Writes. And this is what they heard in the Mission from He-Who-Writes:

"Far have I traveled and many sinners and heathen have I known, but never before have I heard of an instance in which God has been so gravely mocked and insulted as here. A husbandless young woman, not content with having sinned in the ordinary manner, has resorted to the most extraordinary and sacrilegious lie to justify the fruit of her lust. And now she refuses to admit her error and repent. But she shall not drag others with her into perdition! The girl in question is unfit to enter the House of God. Prayer is wasted on her sort. You simple-minded people are no match for a cunning and designing woman, just as your eyes are not trained to spot the Devil, and you must accept the word of one who has come to enlighten you. She is an impostor, and those helping her in her deception, like those that pay heed to lying angakoks, are nothing but idolaters consigned to the eternal flames! Therefore purge yourselves of her, following the advice of the Good Book: 'If your right eye offends you, pluck it out, and cast it from you: for it is profitable for you that one of your members should perish, and not that your whole body should be cast into hell.' Amen."

"Amen," murmured the stunned congregation.

"Somebody always suspected her to be a liar," Padlock immediately confessed to the inner circle of her friends, without even inquiring whether the occasion called for refreshments. "From the first moment there was something about that pregnancy that smacked of sin!"

"She must have met some vagrant outside the village and kept him out of sight, or maybe even killed him in order to gain honor for herself with that fib of virgin birth," said Neghe, who resented having lost her position as first lady of the village to Ivaloo.

"Maybe," old Tippo suggested in a whisper, "she has mated with a bear. Those Northerners do all sorts of things. My mother told me that Northern women are in the habit of consorting with bear and walrus."

"You are nothing but a couple of envious old bitches!" Torngek said.

"You heard the preacher!" her sister rejoined viciously.

"We don't have to believe everything a preacher says," said broad-minded Torngek.

"Who else should we believe? A preacher's knowledge comes straight from God."

"Somebody doesn't know whether his knowledge comes straight from God, but Poopooliluk certainly does."

"It is the voice of the Devil coming from your mouth, Torngek," Tippo screeched, lifting the confabulatory tone of the conversation to a higher key. "You are so filled with sin, with your two husbands, that there is no room for God within you, you wicked woman!"

At this, Torngek struck her amidships, and Tippo went down, yammering like a clubbed seal.

"What is going on?" the preacher asked, coming up in a hurry.

"The Devil has got hold of somebody's sister," Neghe cried. "He puts sinful words into her mouth!"

"Yes," shrieked Padlock. "Torngek is bedeviled and takes Ivaloo's side."

"Already you can see what happens when you allow Satan among you," the preacher said triumphantly. "Impious talk, violence, an old woman assaulted! My aim is to make a peaceful community out of this, but unless you get rid of the evil in your midst you'll call the wrath of

God upon your heads—and God can be terrible in His wrath!"

He himself looked terrible in his wrath, his eyes blazing with an unseemly fire in the dark and narrow face.

CHAPTER THIRTEEN

The Outcast

"**Y**OU bring disgrace on our house and misfortune on our village!" Neghe assailed Ivaloo, finding her in her house when she came back from the sermon.

"What is it all about?" roared Siorakidsok. "Ivaloo has done nothing but cry since she came and won't answer questions." As the white man had brushed past him on the beach and had not asked to meet him, he hadn't gone to the sermon for retaliation, and no one had explained to him what the commotion was about.

"Tetarartee, the new preacher, will not admit us to School and Chapel if we keep company with her," Neghe shouted at him. "He won't give us a Christian marriage when the men come back, nor christen our babies, nor give us tea and keks."

"He won't give us tea and keks?" cried Siorakidsok, outraged.

Neghe pointed a finger at Ivaloo: "This wicked girl has sinned in a most terrible manner, lying about her pregnancy! The sea shall be empty, the land shall be deserted, the women shall be barren if we keep her in our midst. God can be terrible in His wrath!"

"Well then," Ivaloo said wearily, getting off the couch, "somebody will go away from here too."

"Where are you going?" Siorakidsok shouted as if she, not he, were deaf.

"To build a house and stay away from those who fear great harm from the presence of a stupid girl."

"That is a good idea," Siorakidsok said after she had repeated. "But who will feed and clothe you and your brat?"

Ivaloo couldn't help but smile at the old man's simplicity.

"God, of course. The child is His, and He won't let it go hungry or cold."

"What?" Siorakidsok asked.

"God will provide for Poopooliluk," she shouted into his ear, while Neghe shouted into his other ear: "She is full of sin and we shall all be punished if we don't drive her from our midst. Tetarartee said so. How dare she still take the name of God?"

"Quiet, Neghe! If you have sinned, Ivaloo, confess!"

"Somebody must have sinned, otherwise God wouldn't punish her. And a girl would be happy to confess to any sin—but first she should know where and when and how she has sinned."

"An angakok is ready to believe that in your infinite ignorance you have broken some taboo you are not aware of. Each region has its own taboos, and maybe you don't know all the taboos of this region, nor all the white man's taboos."

"Then how can one find out?"

"It is not impossible that an angakok will undertake another trip to the moon," he said in a tone full of resignation. "That's the only way to learn about your sin."

"Your trips to the moon are ended!" broke in Neghe. "Tetarartee has already hinted that we shouldn't heed an angakok if we wish to avail ourselves of the religious services, and nobody will give you any gifts for the Moon Spirit. And a woman thinks this is very good, for the Moon Spirit has been eating a little too many of our supplies lately."

"Get out, Neghe, you old bagful of lice!" shrieked Siorakidsok, frothing. "Somebody wishes to talk alone with Ivaloo."

Neghe went out reluctantly, and Siorakidsok bent forward and said slyly:

"If an angakok can't go to the moon, how can he find out about your sin and set things straight? But maybe you can enlist help to send somebody secretly on a journey."

"Haven't you heard? Nobody wants to associate with a foolish girl any longer," Ivaloo shouted.

"Why do you speak under your breath, silly? There is no one in the house who can overhear us."

"Nobody would listen to somebody now," she yelled into his ear. "Not even Vivi. Besides, it isn't right to cross Tetarartee, who represents God on earth."

"In that case, it is best if you leave the village in a hurry. An angakok doesn't consider sinful what a white preacher considers sinful, but knows only one kind of sin —that which harms the community. So at the present time somebody sees three major offenders: Tetarartee, you and your son. You and Tetarartee, as you spread trouble; and your son as he is the cause of it. And since Tetarartee, besides disposing of tea and keks and other sweets, is also in close alliance with the white man's God, who must be a very dangerous spirit indeed, it is only meet that you and your brat should leave for the common security and well-being."

Ivaloo hung her head. "We'll go."

"It is of no use refusing, you stubborn girl! We'll make you go! But first you should find yourself a provider."

"There is no need, as somebody told you. God will provide."

"Here's what you should do, Ivaloo. Besides you and Vivi there's only a bunch of ugly old hags in our village that nobody would touch except to lay them in their graves. So you should go up to the men and inquire if any-one wants you."

"They all have wives, and according to the latest rules they may not have more than one at a time. Or have you already forgotten?"

"Men are always ready to discard an old wife for a new one. Has nobody asked you?"

"Of course not. They respect a girl because of the way she got Poopooliluk."

"But if you challenge them you'll see that some will take you on, even if you are not yet very fat and strong. Even an angakok might take you on, if he were but two years younger."

Ivaloo cackled. "Thank you, Siorakidsok."

"To the best hunter you say: 'Make your bundles and let us go North, man: as a dowry a girl brings you a male child, and she will make you garments and skin your game, and laugh with you in the long nights till you have tears in your eyes.'"

"Somebody would follow your excellent advice, Siora-kidsok, if it were not for her son. But since he is the child of God and shall be the New Redeemer, somebody wants to dedicate her life to teaching him the Truth, so that he might carry it into the hearts of men, including yours, Siorakidsok. It is a pity that your ears are too hard to let it in."

"Come close, you stupid girl. Somebody wishes to box your ears."

Ivaloo approached respectfully and Siorakidsok gave her a resounding slap. "All angakoks are endowed with a great internal light which reveals to them the real truth!"

"Then why don't you believe in God according to the teachings of the Good Story?" asked Ivaloo, rubbing her cheek.

"An angakok *does* believe, Ivaloo! He believes in every spirit. The world is large, many are the tribes that hunt and fish and sin in it, and there is need for a great many spirits."

"It is obvious now that you were sleeping in School, Siorakidsok! There is only one spirit: the one Jesus has revealed."

"Don't you believe that, Ivaloo. The white men are exceedingly narrow-minded and conceited people, and that's the reason why they dare say there exists, at the most, one spirit—theirs, of course!—and that only he should be obeyed, and all the others thrown away. It isn't so, but to contradict them would be rude, maybe dangerous even. If somebody acts or thinks otherwise than they do, they consider it a sin. Do you know why they don't allow more than one wife or husband? Because none of them would be able to deal equitably with several. If they do borrow other people's wives they do it on the sly, without even asking the husband's permission—that's how contemptible they are! Now, Ivaloo, if these people's god doesn't make you happy, and it would be surprising if he did, but fills you with suffering instead, it means he isn't the god you want. Do you understand?"

Ivaloo wrinkled her nose, which meant No.

"Then listen, stupid. Each tribe has the god it deserves, for gods are made in the image of those that believe in them. Therefore the stupid have a stupid god, the intelligent an intelligent god, the good a good god, the wicked a wicked god. The god of the white men is jealous, selfish and greedy because they themselves are jealous, selfish and greedy. They empty our waters of whale, they empty our seas of seal. Somebody knows them well enough. Many, many years ago, when he was living much farther south, where whale was plentiful because white men were scarce, some white whalers decided to take six Men with them in order to exhibit them before their people who had never seen any Men. Somebody was among those chosen."

"You really were?" Ivaloo said, awed.

"But an angakok was wise enough to decline the invitation, that's why he is still alive today! I had already heard of the sinister hunting grounds of the white men, where the women are idle and force their husbands to do all the work, especially the hard work."

"How shameful!"

"The women beat their male children if they refuse to work, so they all grow up accustomed to hard labor, and terribly afraid of their women, who go about with nothing but mischief on their minds."

Ivaloo leaned back with wide-open eyes and a face of panic. "Nobody has ever heard anything so horrible!"

"No, Ivaloo, not one of those Men came back. Six left on the smoking-boat and were never heard of again. During many years each time we saw a white man we inquired after the Men that had gone to his hunting grounds. Some had heard of the Men's arrival, but then nobody wanted to tell, or knew, what had become of them: they all disappeared without leaving a trace."

A silence followed and Siorakidsok rejoiced in the terror that filled it.

"What did you say?" he asked, because Ivaloo hadn't said anything. "Just listen. The white men's religion is designed to restrain the wickedness of a very wicked people —and a people exceedingly afraid of dying. Their love of their god has been built on their fear of death. Believe me, it takes a white man's soul to bear the burden of the white man's beliefs, not one like yours. Did you understand anything an angakok said?"

"Not a word," she said with admiration.

"Listen, girl. If that Christian God is really such a dangerous and testy Power as Neghe and Tetarartee make him out, then you had better hide from him. But if he is good, as Kohartok used to say, then you have nothing to fear from him. Why should the way to someone who pretends to love you be a stony path that cuts your feet instead of a smooth open road like the ocean? Does he want his children to be happy or to suffer? What do you think?"

"A stupid girl doesn't know the answer."

"Why should he ask self-torture and self-denial which are bound to harden your heart? Why should there be merit in forbearance and abstinence? Can you answer this?"

"No. Somebody doesn't even know what you are talking about."

"An angakok hasn't met, nor wishes to meet, the god of the white men. We always got along very well without him. But an angakok's inner light reveals to him that the spirit who made us Men wants his children to be happy, not unhappy. He doesn't want to see long faces, but glad faces. He doesn't want to hear complaints, but laughter, so he can laugh a little too. And he wants his creatures to be happy because happy people are good, while the unhappy are wicked. Do you understand that?"

Ivaloo wrinkled her nose again.

"Happy people feel like bestowing kindness upon everybody. Only the unhappy will thieve and fight and kill." Siorakidsok made a circular gesture with his hand. "Look around! Here we live in luxury, ease and refinement. This is the comfort of the South. But it isn't your way of life. You will never be happy among the smells of cooking, of tobacco and kerosene, because you are not conditioned to them; nor is your mind conditioned to the teachings of the white preachers. Your body is used to another way of living like your soul to another way of thinking. Here you are a seal bereft of water, an auk bereft of the sky. On the other hand, leave Tetarartee on the ice by himself, and you'll see him die within a turn of the sun for all his hymns and prayers. Of course you don't understand the meaning of all that?"

"Of course not."

"If you try to abide by the white men's ways **you are**

lost, Ivaloo, like they are lost in the land of the Men if they don't have coal and wood. The white men's god has no power to protect them, nor you, on the icy wastes. The great cold paralyzes him, since he is made in the image of the white men. Many white men have always tried, for no good reason at all, to travel in the territory of the Men, with enormous equipment, with huge quantities of coal and stoves, with sleds and dogs and smoking-boats; but their god always left them in the lurch as soon as they had exhausted their supply of coal, and the travels had to be interrupted halfway or ended in disaster. Where the white men reign you are ignorant, Ivaloo, but in your land it is they who are ignorant. So an angakok tells you: go back to the land of the long shadows where you are wise, for there is no sin so great as ignorance, and forget about the white men's god if he is made in their own ugly image —a vengeful and jealous bully who sets a price on salvation and shackle his children instead of releasing them. Flee from a god who says: 'Love Me, or else you will be thrown into a blazing fire.' "

He paused for breath before continuing.

"Your God is a grinning, a joyful, a generous fellow, a mighty hunter who shares the fruit of the chase and laughs with all the women and begets children in every igloo. He doesn't dwell in a stuffy house of wood but on the open ice. He doesn't mind the cold since his belly is full of blubber Don't believe in one who will take vengeance on his own creatures because he made them full of holes and faults! He is a false god, and those advertising such a god are ignorant people or impostors. Do you understand?"

She was crying, wrinkling her nose and shaking her head. "A stupid girl's ears hear your beautiful words, oh Siorakidsok but her heart can't grasp their meaning. There is little understanding in this head and such a great desire to understand. If only there were a way to acquire some of your wisdom!"

"There is, Ivaloo! If you pick some lice from my scalp and put them into your hair, they will pass some of my wisdom onto your head. Help yourself, stupid." And he obligingly bent forward.

"You are too good, Siorakidsok," cried Ivaloo, overjoyed, though hoarse from all the shouting. "Somebody will take but a few, because her head is small, and too much wisdom might give it a terrible ache." And she gratefully followed his advice.

She moved into a tiny house of stone and sod at the foot of a bluff, not far from the village, not very close either, and waited there in Christian resignation for something to happen—she didn't exactly know what. Torngek had enlisted help for the building of the house. Vivi, however, jealously guarded by her mother, had been unavailable.

Ivaloo had retained but few of her former household articles. Even though self-made utensils were the only thing considered personal property and could pass from parents to children, they had to be in use to be respected, and Ivaloo had had no opportunity to avail herself of the ones Asiak had left her, since both the Mission and Siorakidsok's house were fully provided with household implements; so hers had been considered surplus and the members of the community had gradually appropriated them, as need arose.

Torngek gleaned for her what she needed and also gave her a dog for protection—the same husky bitch that had witnessed the birth of her child. She was a valuable bitch because as a pup she had been made to eat a handful of bear nails and a tuft of ermine's hair, thus acquiring the strength of the bear and the boldness of the ermine.

Of food and garments Ivaloo had plenty without having to fish or trap. Not that the villagers gave her anything. Tetarartee, a man of drive and purpose, had put a strong grip on their souls, and no one, not even a black sheep like Torngek, would have dared defy further the wrath of God, much less the wrath of the preacher, by openly supporting an unrepentant sinner ostracized by the Church. But it so happened that when the homebound hunters passed Ivaloo's porch, the straps holding the spoils of the chase would loosen and something would always drop off unnoticed by the carriers. The Finger of God, thought Ivaloo. When a man returned from the hills with a flock of freshly slain auklets on his back a few of the birds would always magically slip off from the lashings. Or someone would carelessly lose a poke of frozen eggs. Someone else, a pair of mittens, and the one time Ivaloo saw it happen and called out to the passers-by, no one seemed to miss them. Or foxhides. Or the white skin of a seal calf, the right thing to make baby boots of. Or the long, smooth sinew from alongside the backbone of the narwhal, which made far better thread than the dog and seal sinews she used to sew with.

And Ivaloo carried her finds inside, smiling knowingly to herself. How could a wise, foolish angakok ever have feared God might abandon her! If he would only trade some of his wisdom for some of her faith. . . .

All summer she had an easy life. She didn't long for the village. She hadn't grown used to crowds. She had a son and a dog for company and they kept her plenty busy. She boiled roots and berries with which to dye her sinew thread, as the village women did; the garments looked so much prettier with colored seams. When she was done with the sewing and feeding she carved little figures and flowers on the handles of her knives, having learned only recently that the animals prefer being killed by handsome weapons, putting up much less resistance.

The vicious little mosquitoes were a blight, sometimes forcing her to stay indoors and smoke them out. Their cloudlike swarms thickened steadily till a snow flurry cleared them away, leaving the air pure and crystalline. Then she might sit outside, watching the hunters go by, watching the kayaks skimming the waves, watching the girls set after berries and fungi and the boys scale the bird cliffs for fledglings that they ate alive, or let decay with all their plumage for a year or two in seal guts crammed with blubber.

The sky was full of birds. The first to arrive had been the little auks in their manifold varieties, followed by the big auks, the seagulls, the guillemots and eider ducks. Now their swarms darkened the sun and the air hummed with the concert of their chirps and cries. Ivaloo strewed morsels of food around a hole she had made in the roof of her house, and when the birds alighted for a peck she would pull them in by their legs, then wring their necks, unless she ate them alive.

When she saw one of the heavy umiaks, filled with whalers, navigate the far waters she stayed indoors, because whales, exceedingly sensitive and self-conscious, are loath to be seen by women while they are being killed. This she had learned during her stay in the South, along with many other things.

Ivaloo felt she was ripening in body and in mind, turning into a woman of vast experience. She was still growing a little, as her clothes betrayed, but she already knew how to take care of herself, as she proved when she lost her house bitch.

The bitch had battled two prowling wolves, till some men from the village, attracted by the uproar, killed one of them and chased the other off. But the bitch had lost an ear in the fight and died a few sleeps later. When the other wolf returned, Ivaloo whetted her snow knife, spread the blade with blubber and stuck the handle into the ground before her porch.

She watched the wolf sniff the baited blade and lick it. Soon it was bleeding from the mouth, but went on licking the blade till it had cut its tongue to ribbons. One sleep later Ivaloo found the prowler stretched out stiffly on the ground. But she knew wolves don't die willingly and that she had to be careful, so she neared silently with her handsomest ax and quickly split the wolf's skull.

From then on she surrounded her house with spring bait and carefully concealed pitfalls.

It was from her father she had learned to get the better of all animals, with the single exception of the wolverine, of course. Not only was she able to kill a bear or a wolf with baited blades; she even knew how to catch the lice on her body by means of a scrap of fur baited with fat that she introduced into her clothes, then pulled out on a string; and she got rid of the elusive fleas, that in summer sprang up from nowhere, by keeping on the floor a couple of fox tails sticky with blood and blubber which attracted the fleas and kept them prisoners.

Yes, she was fully able to take care of herself, with the help of God.

Sometimes a man or a woman stopped casually to exchange a few words. Sometimes Vivi or Torngek dropped in on the sly, bearing small gifts: a dish of mussels, clams or oysters fresh from the seal's stomach, a couple of seal eyes, ptarmigan giblets or other sweetmeats, a sewing needle, a little carved animal of soapstone or some other toy for Poopooliluk.

Although this was not the season for traveling, some wayfarers from afar who had heard of the virgin birth still kept arriving overland, wanting to see her child, and Ivaloo told them what she knew, smiling. They returned her smiles. All were kind to her. Some were Christians, but those came to see her secretly so that Tetarartee might not learn of it.

But she learned plenty about him.

He was at odds with Siorakidsok and kept warning his congregation that to have any doings with an angakok was nothing but rank idolatry entailing everlasting damnation. Siorakidsok, who had lost the support of the community for his trips to the moon, was greatly alarmed by this state of affairs and there was tension in his household between him and Torngek on one side, Neghe and her following on the other.

Neither had Tetarartee brought along any food stores of his own, nor did he try to hunt or fish or do his share of the village work. What Kohartok had left was soon finished, and he accepted with equanimity the meat the villagers brought him, without ever showing himself humiliated by the gifts he received.

Through indefatigable work he had driven the fear of God and the respect for His minister deep into the bones of his flock, and they watched and reported one another incessantly, playing police at the Heavenly Gates. No hunting-on-Sundays. No singing-of-immoral-ballads. No running-naked-round-the-house. No eating-beyond-hunger. No laughing-out-of-wedlock. At any rate, not openly. But prayers, hymns, psalms, sermons, christenings, conversions, marriages, rituals—a one-man show, and edifying to behold.

The religious services had acquired dignity. The faces of the devout were set in seriousness, since Tetarartee would interrupt himself and frown when he saw smiles during the function. Dogs were no longer allowed to participate. And if under Ivaloo's regime, and even Kohartok's, the women suckled their babies during the sermon or put them on the pot that they brought along for that very purpose, now, as soon as a child began to cry or act up, its mother would rush outside with it, followed by Tetarartee's reproachful gaze.

A middle-aged woman from the village, called Meneek, was with child from one of the nomads that had pitched their tents at the cove in the spring and who had recently become a convert. Tetarartee gave the two a tongue-lashing in Chapel and demanded that they get properly married. Meneek didn't like the idea, being the wife of one Kookiak, who had gone with the expedition—and what would happen upon his return? But the preacher guaranteed that nothing would happen, since her union with Kookiak, based on sin, was illegal, giving him no rights other than a seat in Hell; whereas God would smile seeing her wed in proper fashion.

Tetarartee insisted till it would have seemed rude refusing his request any longer; and out of politeness to the white man the couple complied, but with an uneasy feeling.

CHAPTER FOURTEEN

The Return

WINTER brought darkness and the return of the men over the frozen sea.

They had traveled with the expedition so far to the northward over the Glacial Ocean and the big icecap that they had found themselves South again, where the sea also thaws, where there are other white men and smoking-boats. There they had separated from the explorers and returned on their own.

They brought back guns, ammunition, knives and many stories to tell. Two women and several bitches had brought forth on the way, a child had been stillborn and many pups had been devoured by the teams, one white man, frostbitten, had developed gangrene and his legs had to be amputated upon his arrival at the Southern port, and Neghe's eldest son, who had walked back part of the way to look for a forgotten knife, had never been seen again. This was the first news that spread in the village among loud scenes of welcome.

Ivaloo was the last to hear it. She was busy trying to spear fish in a hole she had made in the ocean a little way from her igloo, where the ice was less thick. Lately her supplies had become a little scarce, what with game going south or into retirement and everybody hunting less and sleeping more. The wind kept blowing out her lamp, the moon was down, and by the light of the few available stars it was difficult to lure fish to the surface and still more difficult to sight them when they came.

She had been kneeling by the fish hole for so long with Poopooliluk on her back, and without success, that sheer numbness prevented her from getting up when in the gloom Milak's slender, unmistakable figure loomed up before her. She hadn't heard his footfalls and was struck with terror at the thought that he might be dead and this his ghost bent on mischief.

"Somebody is back from a trip," Milak said casually, as it was fitting for a real man, and his quiet voice dispelled her fears.

"Milak. . . ." She came to her feet with an effort and they shook hands, holding them high above their heads, bowing and grinning. When he tried to rub his nose against hers she warded him off. She was burning to hear about Papik, but if he had passed away on the trip and she would disturb his ghost by mentioning his name the consequences might be disastrous. So she swallowed the question and said instead:

"You say nothing about the child you see on somebody's back. They must have told you about it at the village."

"There was no time to listen to a lot of talk. We just arrived. It is easy to see you have a child. But have you a husband?"

"No," she smiled. "No husband."

"Of course not—or you wouldn't be fishing! And have you meantime found out how inconvenient it is to bend over a hole with a child in you or on you, as somebody foretold?"

"It is not a bit inconvenient. Only once did the child fall out of the jacket hood into the water because some-

177

body bent over forward too much. It gave a girl a small scare and a big laugh. Milak, have you ever heard of the Christian God?"

"Yes, in former travels. Why?"

"This child is His son. Look at him. A girl got him without the help of a man, without even looking at the full moon. He shall be a preacher someday and carry the Truth into the hearts of men."

Milak looked at her, frightened. "Has an evil spirit entered your head? You speak as if you were crazy. Why don't you laugh with somebody instead of speaking nonsense?"

She knitted her brow. "For a long time a girl's body was starved for yours, Milak. She called you in your absence but there was such a lot of ice between us. The heat in my belly was such it could have melted the icecap. It felt as if it might burn a hole inside. But then something came to still somebody's hunger and quench a girl's heat—she was with child."

"But the heat comes back. It always comes back!"

"But one mustn't let it come back. It is a sin." Her gaze ran to and fro over him in quick motions like wind before a storm. They had to stand very close to see each other's eyes in the dark. How she loved the changing sorrows of his features, the thin lines chiseled by thought, for it couldn't be age, the sulky brow and disdainful mouth! It was hard to believe that this frail-looking frame and nervous face had just weathered the blizzards and the seasons, seen blood and violent death.

"You see," she added before he might reply, "somebody's son is everything while she is nothing, because he is the son of God, and the Seed is more important than the soil. A girl wants no more children, so that she may give her whole life to this one, watch over him, teach him, support him."

"Your brain is poisoned by the heat in your belly that

you deny, and that only the heat of man can quench! Frost must be fought with ice, little one, and fire with fire!" He embraced her, squeezing Poopooliluk who started to bawl.

"Somebody didn't want to hurt him," Milak said, abashed.

"It is easy to make him stop," said Ivaloo, sitting down in the snow.

"God's son screams like any other brat," Milak sneered. But presently, watching her pull out her breast and suckle her son, he grew very still.

"Somebody forgot," she smiled, noticing his gaze. "Nobody must look."

"Somebody will show you what must be done!" he cried, angry now.

He snatched the child from her with shaking hands and laid it down in the snow, not heeding its screams. Ivaloo's eyes widened but her lips remained shut. Then he slipped his hand inside her jacket, running it hard over the swollen breasts, one still dripping, and pressed her down on her back.

"A magnificent sinner somebody will make of you!"

She should have kicked and bitten, scratched and spat, as good manners demanded. But there was not a shade of struggle in her: she lay limp and listless, shaking her head in the snow and on the verge of tears. This chilled his ardor and he moved away from her, squatting on his haunches and combing back his hair with trembling fingers.

She sat up and took Poopooliluk into her arms again, cradling him, smiling at Milak. The storm was over.

"In her sleep a girl sometimes dreamed you were laughing with her, for there is no sin in dreaming."

"You should move away from here, away with somebody, Ivaloo!"

"Could we ever fit together, little one?"

"Why not?"

179

"We are so unlike. A girl is stupid, you are clever. She is slow, you are quick. She is from the North, you from the South, which makes you prefer fish while she would rather have meat. To say nothing of her being a woman while you are a man."

"We would fit like bow and arrow, little one! Papik also is sure of it."

"Papik," she cried. "Is he back?"

"You should soon see him."

"Why didn't he come right away?"

"He went to see a woman that is more important to him than his sister."

"How can there be?"

"Can't there?"

"We grew up side by side. We played with the same dolls. Our flesh is the same, from the same seed and the same earth, reared at the same nipples, fed on the same food. A seal? Somebody got the left flipper, he the right. A bear? Somebody got the right eye, he the left. How could there be a more important woman to him?"

"Because time passes and children become grownups who no longer want to play with dolls of horn and fur, but of blood and flesh. So Papik went to see Vivi first, like somebody else came to see you."

She looked at her boots and there was silence, broken suddenly by the furious barking of her new dog at the igloo.

"Somebody is coming!" She got up quickly and hastened home with her child in her arms, followed by Milak.

She found her beaten dog whimpering in the entrance, her lamp already lit, and on the snow couch a big figure, a broad face with the grin of large teeth, eaters of raw meat, and here was the very image of Ernenek, just as Asiak had seen him a generation ago.

"Papik, little one!" Ivaloo cried and rushed to embrace him.

So little was he that though he bent his head the tips of his unruly hair scraped the ice of the vault. He was a mass of muscles, broader and taller than upon his departure, and there was that arrogant tug of the underlip, that sudden thrust of the jowl, and those blunt movements of the chest, that had been Ernenek's.

She rubbed her face against his and poked her nose in his cheeks and snuffed at him. Her eyes filled with tears, but not from grief. This was Papik, her flesh, her blood; this was Ernenek reborn, this was Asiak continued. In the odor of his face, in the blending of his breath and her breath, she smelled again the air of her childhood and their first igloos.

And she knew also that he hadn't come to prate and eat and rest, but to ask, and that it was urgent, and that he was angry.

She recognized the smell of anger on his skin.

"It came to pass that somebody has returned," Papik said, dropping heavily back onto the couch.

"It came to pass that somebody begot a child in your absence." She went at him again, snuffing and rubbing. Flat faces rubbed easily.

Papik lifted the child in the air and laughed at it as at an excellent joke. He had forgotten about his worry. One thing at a time.

"What a strange-looking child. Hair and eyes like white men have."

"That's because Poopooliluk comes from the white men's God. Somebody will explain it to you some other time. First tell a sister what is the matter with you, Papik. There is trouble on your mind."

He put down the child and picked up his worry.

"Ivaloo," he said with a scowl, "somebody has been thinking."

"And what came of it?"

"An ache in the head, mainly, and at the end a conclusion. After two years with the white men somebody understands them less than at the first meeting. Their ways are not the ways of the Men, Ivaloo. Your brother hasn't grown used to them, as some have. And now we have heard that Tetarartee has driven you from the village. So somebody has decided to live where there are no white men, to take you back where the sun is low and there are animals that have never seen human beings."

"Maybe it is a good conclusion, little one."

Milak laughed bitterly. "You can't escape white men by going North! Not any more. You know that, Papik. No, no. Better be friends with them, learn their trade, even try learning their rules."

"Why can't you escape by going North?" asked Ivaloo.

"Because they are coming North, too. They told us. Didn't they, Papik?"

Papik nodded. "It is true. But let them come! Somebody will make keener knives and faster arrows and longer spears, and prepare a lot of spring bait, and when they come they shall be killed like wolves!"

"Why do they come if they don't like the cold and the long nights? And if they want oil they get it more easily where the sea melts."

"There are two things they want besides oil," Milak began, and it became very quiet in the igloo. "First, a certain metal that is supposed to be hidden under the Northern icecap. So they are preparing to come with a lot of explosives—that is the thing bullets are made of—and blast the icecap, and then dig for the metal they hope to find in the earth beneath the ice."

"What do they want with so much metal? Haven't they a lot of metal already?"

"It is a special metal they need for the making of another, very potent explosive, with which it is easy to kill a large number of people at once. That metal is scarce in their land, but according to their angakoks they will find it under our ice in large quantities."

"Explosives to kill people?"

"White men kill one another regularly, every so often. Isn't that what they told us, Papik?"

Papik nodded darkly and Ivaloo looked from one to the other in amazement.

"It seems," said Milak, "that a great frenzy assails them every so many years, and then great tribes unite to destroy other great tribes. On such occasions they kill more people than the Men kill caribou."

"But why?"

"It seems it has to do with their trade. But it was too complicated for the white men to explain, and they couldn't agree in their explanations. It almost started a fight among them."

"All this is very confusing. You don't explain well."

"They didn't explain well either. But they made it very plain that many white men would come North, blast the ice, dig for metal, and remain there whether they found some or not."

"Why?"

"That's the second reason for their coming: to prevent other tribes of white men from settling there. It seems the first to set foot there will have an advantage over the others during their next killing frenzy."

Ivaloo was dropping from surprise to surprise. "But have they never heard of the teachings of Jesus Christ? Have they no preachers in their land?"

"Maybe their preachers are too busy traveling in the land of the Men," Milak said. "Anyway, they are planning to go North. First they send preachers, then traders, then men with explosives. It seems they always do that."

"For the time being the North is free of them, and a man intends to go back there," Papik said stubbornly. "But it happens that somebody finds it tiresome always having to ask other men for the loan of a wife. They feel so important, even if they get handsomely rewarded with a piece of hunt."

Milak assented strongly. "It means such a loss of face. Somebody also would rather lend than borrow a wife."

"Both things are wrong," Ivaloo said.

"Why?"

"Nobody knows why, but so it is. The white man says it, and he knows exactly what is right and wrong."

"How do you know that he knows?" asked Papik.

"He says it."

"Oh. Meanwhile, as a consequence of thinking somebody has decided to take a wife before going back North."

"There is Vivi," Ivaloo put in casually. "She is a good seamstress."

"A man has heard that on the trip. So he went to her parents and offered them a new steel knife for her. But first he asked to see her sewing." He wished to make it clear that convenience only commanded his action, not any other feeling which would have been undignified for a man.

"Somebody has seen a lot of her needlework," Ivaloo said. "She will make a good wife."

"However, her mother, Padlock, not only refused to let me see any of her work, but rejected my proposal altogether, for reasons, it seems, that concern the wishes of Tetarartee. Now all this seems very strange."

"You see, Tetarartee, who knows more about sin than anybody we ever met, tells us what may be done and what may not be done, according to the wish of God."

"What God?"

"The most powerful spirit of all, more powerful than all other powers and spirits combined, and very courageous. He is not even afraid of the ghosts of the dead, but roasts them over a big fire if they break the taboos He has set up."

Papik puckered his forehead. "During our absence the women have been taught to say and do a lot of things that the men can't understand. So Kookiak can't explain why his wife Meneek is hiding from him. It seems the white man has encouraged someone else to steal her from him. And Argo is at odds with Neghe. And Padlock has said that before her husband Hiatallak may laugh with her they must see the preacher and get his permission. No man can swallow such humiliations! The village women and all those strangers that have recently settled speak of sinfulness and of the white man's taboos. The white men we traveled with taught us only one taboo: we were not permitted to touch their belongings. However, somebody was told by Vivi's mother that you can explain what the white man wants before giving his permission. Somebody may give it to him, if it is not too humiliating."

Ivaloo nodded. "He wants everybody to become Christians. Now Vivi's mother, Padlock, is a very good Christian, and so is Vivi, and she can marry nobody but a Christian. Is that clear?"

"No," said Papik.

"Yes," said Milak. "Somebody has heard a lot of that in former travels."

"Any woman will marry a good hunter," Papik said impatiently. "Somebody can hunt. Vivi can sew. What has the white man to do with it? Is he going to hunt for her?"

"You don't seem to understand, Papik. We try to respect the taboos he has set up."

"Does he respect our taboos?"

"No. He doesn't believe in them."

"Then why do you believe in his?"

"Somebody believes in all taboos, little Papik. Personally, she is very fond of taboos. To her, the more taboos, the better."

"What is the solution?"

"One good solution is that you become a Christian."

"How do you go about it?"

"You must find faith."

"Where does it occur? In the mountains, ice or water? Do you trap it, hunt it or fish it?"

"It occurs in your own heart, after you have taken lessons. You must listen to the Good Story, and learn to love everybody, even your enemies, do good to them that hate you, and forgive those that hurt you. These are the teachings."

"All this sounds extremely stupid to a man."

"It won't, after you let the Christ enter your heart, like somebody did."

"Did it hurt?"

"What?"

"When this thing got into your heart? It must hurt."

"No, Papik. It fills you with sweetness."

"So if you don't take revenge, and love your enemies, you are a Christian."

"If the preacher says so."

"Is he a Christian?"

"Of course he is."

"Then why doesn't he forgive you for whatever you did to him?"

"Maybe we are supposed to forgive only our enemies, not our friends."

"But what did you *do?*"

Ivaloo frowned. "A girl is too ignorant to know, Papik. Maybe she must atone for not going to Chapel during all the years before meeting Kohartok. Or because her parents were sinners. Someday she will find out the reason, maybe. You see, we are stupid, he is intelligent."

"But why doesn't he love you, if he says one should love everybody? And he doesn't love you, Ivaloo! Padlock made that plain."

"Oh Papik, don't ask so many questions! You will never become a good Christian if you do. Somebody has been thinking and thinking about these things till her head hurts, like yours. We live in a mysterious world! A girl never knew how mysterious it was till the white men began explaining it."

"Oh Ivaloo! Your brother has been told you are crazed, and he begins to believe it! There isn't a word of sense in what you say. You shouldn't have been left alone!"

And the silence that followed was filled with the thought of Asiak, of whose death Papik could only just have learned. After sitting a little in silence he said:

"Mother used to tell us: 'White man is like a plague, and only in the very great cold is one safe from it.' That is why we must go so far north that wherever we look we'll be looking south, and kill anybody who wants to come after us!" His anger was waxing hot, fanned by his own words. "Ivaloo," he said, leaping to his feet, "there is the taste of blood in my mouth! Padlock said Vivi may not even talk to me before having the white man's permission. Ivaloo, somebody is going to ask for that permission, and the white man had better give it!"

Milak sprang up too. "Somebody will go along. He also has things to say to the white man!"

It was Ivaloo's turn to spring up. "Excuse a foolish girl for being forward," she said, covering the exit, "but somebody will talk to him before you do. No good can come of wrath. Have tea meanwhile."

"But hurry," Papik said. "A man doesn't feel like tea. He feels anger, and can't stop it any more than the growth of his hair."

His hands shook, and the heat of his anger inflamed Milak too.

"We'll wait a short while," Milak said. "Then we'll come —with guns."

"But have tea, first." Hastily she put snow to melt over the lamp, strapped the child on her back and left running.

A light shone through the window of the Mission but the door was bolted. Kohartok had never bolted the door.

"Knock, and it shall be opened," Ivaloo reminded herself by way of encouragement, and knocked.

"Who is it?"

"Ivaloo."

She heard the snick of the lock and Tetarartee let her in. A book lay open on his chair under the kerosene lamp. "What is it?" His face was haggard and she felt pity for him. He must be suffering. But his blazing eyes asked for no pity.

"There is something you should know," Ivaloo said. "Dreadful things are happening in this world. A girl just learned that among white men a great frenzy breaks out every so often. They kill each other off in great numbers on such occasions, and soon they are coming up North to look for some metal with which to kill more people."

Tetarartee scowled. "Is that what you came to tell me?"

"A silly girl thought you ought to know, so you may put an end to it."

Tetarartee tapped the floor with his foot. "You are very kind to inform me."

"Oh, a girl did it gladly!"

"Is there anything else you think an ignorant preacher ought to know?"

"Yes. That somebody's brother, Papik, who has just returned, wishes to go back North with her."

"Are you taking back the story of your virgin pregnancy before you leave?" Tetarartee said balefully.

"And heap the sin of lying on top of all a girl's other sins? Certainly not, Tetarartee."

"Then go, go back with your brother, Ivaloo, and may God have mercy on your soul!"

"Thank you, Tetarartee. It is the first time you have said a kind word to a foolish girl. We'll leave at once. But it happens that Papik is planning to take Vivi with him, women being scarce up North. Will you marry them in the sight of God before they leave?"

"I have already been informed about who came back and what they are, and your brother appears to be as remote from Christianity as you. But I am willing to talk to him, in the hope that my words will fall on more receptive ground than with you."

"You always speak very beautifully, Tetarartee. But now a stupid girl would like to know what you said."

"Papik will have to take many lessons before I can pronounce him a Christian and give him a Christian marriage."

"But there is no time for any lessons! If you marry them now, somebody will teach him everything he has to learn. She knows the Good Story well, and also the way to his heart."

"A liar like you, enlightening someone with the Truth? Poor girl, will you never stop talking nonsense?"

"It so happens," Ivaloo said with a thread of voice, "that Papik is going to leave with Vivi anyway, and if you don't give them a Christian marriage they will go without it and live in sin."

"So that's the sort of brother you have! Worthy of his sister, indeed! How could I declare such a fellow a Christian?"

"Please, oh please, to avoid violence and trouble!"

"Threats of the Devil shall be of no avail in the House of God." Tetarartee spoke coldly now, but with glowing intensity beneath the ashes. "Take your brother and your brood with you, and don't come back till God shows you the way to grace by entering your heart! Go, now. You have caused enough harm in our midst."

Ivaloo frowned. "A girl has so prayed to God for guidance, and it came to pass that He is now showing her the right path. If she ever wants to perceive Him again she must not listen to you, for all you put in her heart is hatred and bitterness. Siorakidsok was right: there are many gods, and your god is not Kohartok's god. Somebody hasn't felt Him in her heart ever since you arrived, Tetarartee, for He wouldn't come near where you are. But now a girl knows where to find Him!"

"Get out, you monstrous blasphemer!" cried he, showing her the door.

But she had already turned her back on him, and was running.

Into Padlock's igloo she rushed. Padlock was queen here and Hiatallak, her husband, nothing but a servant, though both had always tried to conceal the fact before the community. They didn't look like a couple long separated and glad to meet again. They were as far apart as possible, their faces in a storm. Vivi was between them. Her tear-reddened eyes lit up on seeing Ivaloo.

"Forgive a forward girl for entering uninvited and talking unasked," Ivaloo said quickly, "but there is a brother who is willing to give you anything you want in exchange for Vivi. He is usually fortunate as a hunter."

"What did Tetarartee say to that?" Padlock asked severely.

"He wants to take his time about it and Papik doesn't. So if an impertinent girl might advance an opinion it might be better to let him have her anyway, and later, after he has been taught the Good Word, he can become a Christian."

"Are you crazy, girl?"

"Oh, everybody calls somebody crazy, so she must be, but some say it for one reason, others for the opposite reason. One thing is certain though: Papik is coming to get Vivi and there will be trouble unless you let her go."

"Let him come," said Padlock, a wall of defiance. "For the sake of our child's soul we shall fight him to our last breath. Won't we, Hiatallak?"

Hiatallak nodded with a sheepish grin, scratching his

head and wondering what it was all about. Vivi kept her head very straight, her gaze anchored on Ivaloo's face.

"Will you come to Papik if he wants you, little one?" Ivaloo asked.

Vivi reddened. Her eyes ran to her mother, quailed, then she said quickly, with a breath of voice, "Yes."

Padlock struck her daughter to the ground, leaving her whimpering. Ivaloo, who had never seen parents strike their children, stood terrified. Padlock turned on her like a fury:

"Get out and don't show yourself again, you wicked girl! Somebody believes, indeed, it was none but the Devil himself who made you that child you are carrying on your back!"

But Ivaloo wasn't listening. Padlock's anger reminded her of the anger she had left brewing in her own igloo. She rushed out and hurried homeward. She was getting tired of running. Poopooliluk lay heavy on her back. Now he woke and began to cry.

Her igloo was empty, the wick spluttering and near death, the water on the lamp untouched.

Outside again, her knees gave way, from weakness, from fear, and from not knowing which way to turn. Everything came back to her that Asiak used to tell, filling her with anguish. The Men were going to do violence, and the white men would be after them, for years on end, and poison their lives with the threat and the dread of their might and write their names into big books that outlast memory.

She trekked back heavily over the sea toward the settlement. Several times she had to stop to regain her breath. All the igloos were lit, glowing in the night. Everybody was up, celebrating the return. But something seemed to be afoot. The settlement was alive with the flare of tallow torches flitting about, casting long wavering shadows, and she quickened her step.

Argo shot past her with a flaming flare in one hand, a gun in the other.

"What is it, Argo? Why aren't you home with Neghe after the long absence?" she called, trying to keep up with him.

"Blood is flowing, and there will be more! Kookiak has just slaughtered the man who had stolen his wife, Meneek, and somebody's own wife, Neghe, has been bewitched by the white man so she won't allow her own husband within laughing distance! She went to the wood house for protection. And she will need protection, the tailless bitch! A husband intends to club her till she'll feel like laughing once more."

"Wait, wait!" Ivaloo cried in vain.

There was the fall of more heavy boots in the snow, and Papik and Milak loomed up beside her. Both carried guns and were heading for the Mission.

"Papik! Where are you going?"

There was battle lust in Papik's voice. "Since you weren't coming back we went to get our guns, and on the way we learned that Padlock had taken shelter in the white man's house, dragging Vivi with her. Now somebody is going to get Vivi out."

Ivaloo could barely keep up with her brother's stride. Flares, footfalls and voices were converging from all sides. Argo was ahead, and Torngek's husbands came carrying Siorakidsok in his rug.

"Drive the white devil back where he came from!" Siorakidsok was calling. "This is the end of his evil influence!"

On shore, before the Mission porch, old Tippo's shadow suddenly rose. "Get back, you wicked people!" She also was brandishing a gun. The village seemed full of guns since the return of the expedition. "Don't you dare desecrate the House of God!"

"Shut your big mouth lest we see your feet, you toothless seal cow," shrieked Siorakidsok.

"Put away that gun, Tippo," said Argo, brushing past her. "It may go off, you silly woman."

"Yes, in your back, if you don't turn about at once!"

But Argo strode on.

Papik overtook him and leaped up to the porch of the Mission. "Out with Vivi, white man, or you have lived your days," he boomed, hammering the door with the butt of his gun.

"Somebody wants to see the color of your liver, Tetarartee!" Milak called out in his high, clear voice.

"Do him a favor and bounce him into Heaven," came Siorakidsok's high falsetto.

A shot rang out and Argo, who had already one foot on the Mission porch, changed his mind. He put a hand to his side, tumbled down and lay motionless, his flare fizzling in the snow.

"Keep off, you heathen!" cried Tippo, waving the smoking gun like a flag.

"Kill the crazy old bitch!" screeched Siorakidsok. "Kill her like a wolverine! Tear her guts out!"

"Help!" Tetarartee's voice rang from within the Mission. "All good Christians and men of good will, join in the fight against the Devil!"

Ivaloo caught up with her brother and tried to pull him back. Shots were ringing. Papik, veins swelling on his throat, kept hammering away at the door, with Ivaloo hanging from his arm, but the door stood fast.

Then from below, Milak started. He flashed forth like a streak of light, leaped onto the porch and at full speed landed squarely upon the door. It gave way like snow under the impact and he crashed headlong inside, sweeping Papik with him. Ivaloo was quick to follow.

With a gun in his hands the preacher stood in the far corner, pale, but straight and defiant, covering Vivi and Neghe, flanked by Padlock and Hiatallak. Padlock was clutching a spear.

"Get behind me, Satan!" thundered Tetarartee, taking a step forward and fidgeting with his gun.

Papik was too proud to take notice of him. He flung his own gun and a knife on the floor at Padlock's feet.

"You take this, Padlock," he said, managing to sound quiet, "and somebody shall take Vivi in exchange," and, Ernenek all over, he walked unarmed into a leveled gun and a woman's claws.

"Get hence, Satan," cried Padlock, hurling her spear. Papik saw it clearly, but ducking before a woman would have been below his dignity and he made no move to avoid it. It ripped a gash in his cheek and landed with a thud in the wall behind. Papik went ahead, blood streaming from his face.

Tetarartee seemed to have his gun ready at last, but before he could fire it Padlock had descended with her fists upon Papik, covering him, and by the time Papik had knocked her down, Milak had swung into action again.

Swift as lightning but silent as sunshine he weaved through the wavering and groping people, snatched the gun from the preacher's hands and smashed it over his head again and again, and then again after he had floored him, till Ivaloo threw herself under his blows. Then he turned about, white and shaking, and began to smash the gun on everything in sight.

Meantime in Papik, also, wrath was boiling over.

He picked up his knife from the floor and slashed away at the books, the pictures, the pots and pans and bottles. Then he cut the lamp from the ceiling. It tumbled to the floor with a crash, and darkness was in the room for a moment till, kindled by the dying wick, the spreading kerosene caught fire.

The flames worked magic on Papik and Milak, stopping their tremor and slaking their thirst. They had never seen such a fire, and it held them fascinated and spellbound. But from Hiatallak came a great howl of fright and he bolted out, followed by Padlock and Neghe. Through the open door came a gust of air, the flames hissed and spread, tidal waves of heat melted the grease on the faces and seared their skin, and Papik came back to reality.

"Come, Vivi. Somebody's sled is ready and somebody's dogs are lean and fast. Come, Ivaloo. Come, Milak. Let us make a run. There is shooting outside, and they may hit us because it is too dark to aim." He was really cool now, and no wrath. Calmly he took Vivi's hand and pulled her out of the house.

"Somebody is going ahead to get his sled ready by your igloo," Milak said to Ivaloo. "His dogs are fast and lean, too." And off he went.

The fire had already half the wooden flooring and was still gaining ground, filling the room with smoke. Ivaloo knelt down by Tetarartee and shook him.

"Can you get up?" she asked, coughing.

He blinked at her, moaning, a trickle of blood running from his head into his beard. "You are Satan incarnate," he said brokenly. "Without you this would be a peaceful community. We have you and your kind to thank for what is happening."

"But we don't want any thanks."

"Go back where you belong!"

"Yes, that's where we are going!" Ivaloo said joyfully. "But you must move. The flames are very close to you." She helped him on his feet and rushed out.

Below the porch she stumbled over Argo lying in a pool of blood. Neghe was on the ground beside him, wailing, shaking his head and calling his name. Farther off, Tippo, face in the snow, was giving forth her last shivers. Otherwise the expanse before the Mission was deserted. A few flares, abandoned because they made too easy targets, were sizzling in the snow, and the unfamiliar, acrid smell of gunpowder lay heavy in the breathless air.

Wrath had spread like a plague. The holy war was on. From behind the igloos shots and shouts rang out. But Christians and heathens were shooting mainly to keep their mittens warm, for it was too dark to aim.

Ivaloo walked swiftly toward her igloo. A few bullets whizzed about her, but not for a moment was she afraid of being hit. She was glad the child was quiet.

"Hunt them down and root them up, the sinners, the heathens, the thieves!" thundered Tetarartee's voice, and glancing over her shoulder Ivaloo saw him tall and black in the doorframe of the Mission against the background of fire. "Rope them in and wipe them out, the assassins, the brood of the Devil, the scum of Hell!"

She was at the end of her strength but kept up her smart pace till the din of battle faded into the past. It was warm, the wind had fallen, the stars had disappeared and in the air was the hint of snow, that's why the sounds didn't carry far.

Above, the overcast sky was bleeding with the reflection of the fire.

Milak was cuffing the surly dogs that were in open revolt because they saw the whip instead of the food they had anticipated.

"Papik and Vivi have already left," he said. "We will follow their tracks."

"Did you take the household goods from my igloo?"

"Yes, little one."

"Did you harness the bitches in heat on the longest traces, so that the following dogs might pull for all they are worth?"

"It has been done, little one," he shouted joyfully.

"And the pregnant ones on the shortest traces, to prevent their teammates from swallowing their litters? We'll need new dogs."

"Of course, Ivaloo! Now step aboard, and a man will untangle the team!"

But she didn't obey. The team was in a turmoil, all in one heap, clawing, snapping and snarling, the dogs over the bitches, the bitches fighting one another, and under Milak's admiring gaze, for few women knew how to handle a team, she snatched the heavy stick out of his hand and cracked down on them—and one could hear the dismal thud of bones being struck between one yelp and the next —and after they were straightened out she cracked down on them anew while giving the command of departure, and they started tearing with such force that if the sled hadn't advanced, the sea would have backed up. Then she jumped aboard in front of Milak and grabbed the whip with the short wood handle and the long lash of sealhide to see whether she still knew how to wield it against the wind all the way down to the leader.

She did.

As their eyes grew adjusted to the gloom the landscape began to emerge against the night. They were heading for the dark horizon of the sea fields in Papik's tracks. Ivaloo, hot from the exertion, put down the whip, and inhaled deeply, savoring the air fragrant with the promise of snow. With a dozen breaths she had recuperated her strength.

"Milak," she cried joyfully, drinking the wind, "why was a girl away from a sled so long? She is breathing again, and feels full of goodness, with not a drop of the bitterness of which there was a lot lately. Somebody is happy, Milak, looking forward to the igloo we'll build when we are tired, and in the igloo she'll look forward to the harnessing of the team upon rising. But will you be happy up there, Milak?"

"A man can always come back South if he is not."

"No you can't, Milak."

"Why not?"

She paused a space before she spoke. "You have killed Tetarartee, little one—and you know the white men will never forgive you, and that your name will be in their books forever."

"Are you sure he is dead?" said Milak without a trace of concern.

"Dead, and roasted. A girl saw him with her own eyes."

And she paused, reflecting that she had learned, at last, how to lie.

"Well then," said Milak with a shrug in his voice. "It will save us the bother of ever returning South. But are you still determined not to laugh? For somebody is determined to make you, little one, if he has to beat you all the colors of the sunset!"

"I told you the reason by the fishing hole, Milak, little one. In long lonely nights a girl has prayed God for a Sign, and He answered with this child that is now sleeping so quietly. It is too clear a sign! So if we find a spot up North that the white men won't reach, there one will raise this son in the Truth and from there, if his Father wills, he shall some day set forth: 'to prepare the way of God, make His paths straight.'"

"Sometimes it sounds as if it is not you talking, Ivaloo, but some mad foreign spirit that has entered your body!"

Ivaloo laughed. "At times a stupid girl must use words from the Good Book to express her thoughts. But some day Poopooliluk shall word what his ignorant mother can only feel. He will be the savior that white men, as somebody now knows, are sorely in need of."

Milak made no reply and Ivaloo cracked the whip to fill the silence with something besides the breathing of the team.

"If God doesn't wish Poopooliluk to follow in the tracks of His other Son as we follow in Papik's tracks; if He thinks people unworthy of a new savior because they ignore the teachings of the first—well then, He will give another Sign, telling so. Don't you see?"

"Oh Ivaloo, little one," cried Milak within himself, distressed, for he had already seen the Sign: Ivaloo's trundle hood was one big patch of blood, and over its rim Poopooliluk's head lolled loosely—his lips parted, his nostrils pinched, the sky of his eyes befogged.

Ivaloo's happy voice startled Milak out of his musing:

"It has started to snow! The blood of the dead is beginning to fall. Now nobody can track us."

"But the snow will cover also Papik's tracks, and we'll lose him if he hasn't stopped."

"It is not impossible that Papik knows what to do."

They strained in the dark. The team was sniffing the air, yelping, and presently the barking of other dogs answered through the night.

"It came to pass that they have stopped," Milak cried exultantly.

"And snow is falling heavy," said Ivaloo, opening her mouth towards the sky to receive the blood of the dead.

The snow was falling, covering their tracks.